Book Four Clover Series

Danielle Stewart

Copyright Page

An *Original* work of Danielle Stewart.
Facing Home Copyright 2014 by Danielle Stewart

ISBN-13: 978-1511851022
ISBN-10: 1511851023

Cover Design by Gin's Book Designs
(GinsBookDesigns.com)
Stock Photo Attribution Couple: Couple: stockasso(Andrea De Martin) / DepositPhotos
Landscape: lola19 (Gordan Jankulov) / Depositphotos Inc.

Dedication

To Benita, Denny and Hemi Kay:

Thank you for your contribution to this book. I could not have written it without your guidance.

That is a small thank you compared to the enormous gratitude I have for your service to this country. Because of you and your fellow service people, my family is able to choose what religion we practice. We are able to send our child to the school we choose. Because you sacrifice, we are free.
I was naive to so much of what a military family, as well as returning soldiers, experience. Thank you for the education

For the rest of my readers remember to thank a veteran today! Whether online or in person.

To all the military families and personnel out there - THANK YOU.

Synopsis

Vitorino "Click" Coglinaese shouldn't feel more at home in a war zone than he does in his own backyard. But when you earn yourself a nickname like Click, *the only sound the enemy hears before you strike,* transitioning back to civilian life is a more insurmountable task than any combat mission. Click knows his family is longing for the kid who left for boot camp six years ago, but now he finds himself feeling like a stranger amidst his loved ones. The only thing strong enough to pull him back to Sturbridge, Tennessee is knowing one of his four sisters is in trouble.

Can Click fight his nightmares and haunting memories long enough to save his sister? Can Jordan, the woman he loves, help him navigate his way toward peace with his family? Or will facing home be the one fight Click can't win.

Chapter One

<u>Jordan</u>

I thought I was prepared. I spent the entire car ride from Clover, North Carolina, to Sturbridge, Tennessee, memorizing names and trying to remember which children belonged to which of Click's sisters. I tried to brace myself for the warnings Click had given me. *Everyone might sound like they're yelling, but really, that's just how they talk. If my mother offers you food, take it. There is no amount of turning her down that will work.* I've planned to gain five pounds. I can hit the gym hard when all this is sorted out.

As we pass a sign welcoming us to Sturbridge I realize there's no turning back. I'm committed now. Whatever's waiting here for Click, we'll face it together. But I'm still scared. That's not something I often admit, not even to myself.

As we get closer to our destination, I slip my pinky over the latch of the car door and contemplate opening it. Could I hit the ground running and hope Click keeps driving? Probably not. He's too much of a gentleman for that. He'd feel obligated to stop and pick me up off the pavement.

"You look nervous." Click smirks, patting my thigh gently. "They're going to love you. And if they don't, they'll be happy enough to see me that they'll probably leave you alone."

"I don't make a great first impression." I clear my throat as I flip down the mirror on the visor for the hundredth time and check between my teeth. "I tend to come off as a little . . ." I pause not knowing the right word.

"I know you do," Click agrees, seemingly aware there might not be a good adjective to describe me. He flips the mirror closed and softens his eyes empathetically. "It doesn't matter what you look like, so stop worrying. They don't judge people based on appearances."

"That's good to know." I nod my head, trying to convince myself. Click is the first guy who's taken me home to meet his family, and I don't want to screw that up. Knowing they won't critique me based on superficial things is putting me at ease.

"Yeah, appearances don't matter to them. They'll judge you on how much you eat, how well you cook, and how many kids you plan to have."

"They'll watch how much I eat, like health food wise?"

"No, I should say they'll watch what you don't eat. It's an insult if you turn down food, and being thin is somehow equated with being rude. You have to understand, we've always stuck out like a sore thumb here in the South. My parents are a couple of first and second generation Italians. Showing up in a small town like Sturbridge, they didn't exactly fit in. Everyone kept saying, *Just give them time. Before you know it the Coglinaeses will be adapting to life here in Tennessee.* And do you know what happened?"

"You acclimated and everything worked out?" I ask hopefully as I try to read Click's expression.

"No, my parents turned our neighborhood into Little Italy. They launched a take-no-prisoners push of their ideals and traditions. My family doesn't mold into their surroundings, they force the backdrops of the world to change in order to match them."

"Why isn't this making me feel any better?"

"Oh come on, big bad Jordan isn't afraid of anything. She's a tiger," Click teases as he brushes my hair off my shoulder.

"Yes, at work I was, but that's because I didn't care what people thought of me. This is different. Very different."

"Why do you care what they think of you? You know who you are and so do I. I happen to love that person. So forget what they think."

"That's easy to say but they are your family, and I'm hoping to be around you for a while—*if you're lucky*—and that means I'll be around them. It would be easier if they liked me."

"Let me put your mind at ease: I don't plan on staying in Tennessee. I'm going to help out whichever one of my sisters is in trouble and then move to somewhere else. I don't belong back here."

"They're your family. Like a huge, tons-of-kids, big-dinners-every-Sunday family. How can you already decide you don't want that in your life anymore?"

"Do you know why I was home a total of twenty-nine hours before I took off and ended up in Clover? I can't be who they want me to be. I'm not happy about that, but it's reality. They're all remembering the kid who left and aren't comfortable with the stranger who's come home."

"You didn't give them much time to get comfortable with him. I'm positive they must miss you. I'm sure they just need time to adjust, and so do you."

"Adjust to what?" Click asks, and I see his grip on the steering wheel tighten. "You don't flip this stuff off like a switch. I'm programmed. Something happens and I react. A loud noise, I'm tackling you to the ground to protect you. I'm always on. That's why Clover worked for me. I needed to be this guy." He slaps his hand to his chest. "None of that exists in Tennessee for me. No one needs me to use the skills I have or live in my mindset. They want me to be something I don't know how to be anymore."

"So you plan to live in a constant state of danger in order to feel like yourself?" I almost don't want to hear his answer. I don't want to think of him as always needing to risk his life to be happy.

"I have no idea. I didn't think you had much of a plan either." He says this almost like an accusation, and I feel bad for bringing any of it up. I know he's stressed about going home and not knowing what he's up against. His father called and told him his sister needed help, but didn't give any more detail than that. The last thing I need to do is add to that unknown.

"Being back here should be nice. You should be able to relax." I'm trying to put him at ease as I reach my hand across to touch him, but I can sense his tension and slight recoil. I'm saying the wrong thing, even though I don't mean to.

"It's not like I can just go put my ass in a hammock and daydream my life away. My mind isn't really some calm oasis right now."

"What do you mean?" I ask, seeing his stress level grow higher than I've seen it before. Going home to be with his family makes him more on edge than anything we encountered in Clover, including gunfire and imminent danger.

"Nothing. It's complicated. All I'm saying is, I do better when I'm challenged, when I put into action all the things I've learned. Being back home reminds me of everything I'm not anymore. My mother has always been overbearing and she can't understand why I don't pour my heart out to her about what it was like being deployed. She wants to know every detail. She wants to help me work through stuff, but it drives me crazy. It's like the Spanish Inquisition every time I talk to her, so I don't talk to her much anymore. My dad is the opposite, completely silent about it. He acts like I was at summer camp instead of in a war zone. And while I prefer that over my mother's approach, it still grates on me. My choices are having someone ignoring where I've been for the last six years or acting like I'm a grenade with the pin pulled and could blow up any minute."

"Parents can mean well but miss the mark." I'm trying to soften the tension that's building. "You have your sisters. They must understand things better than your parents. No generation gap."

"My sisters think I'm an elitist, or something along those lines. They assume missing their weddings or their kids' christenings were choices I made deliberately to hurt them. Like I checked out of our family because I felt like it. It's tense and, like I said, complicated. I'm still readjusting to civilian life; I don't need that pressure."

I contemplate driving my point further. I can see where his family is coming from. I've been on the naïve side of understanding the motivations of someone in the military. Frankly, I was a downright bitch about it when we met. Click and I started on rocky ground on this topic ourselves, so I clam up. I'm here to support him and give him something to ground himself to, not to gang up on him.

"I just want to get to the bottom of whatever mess one of my sisters got herself into and then get out of here."

It's odd his father wouldn't tell him what was going on over the phone. He wouldn't even tell Click which of his sisters was in trouble. I'm worried this was a ploy to get him home, and Click won't take that well.

"That's fine." I touch his shoulder and am relieved it has now relaxed. "I'm here for you. Whatever you want." As we pull onto a quiet dirt road I can tell by the five cars spilling from the driveway this is Click's house. They've all gathered, just like he warned they would. The welcoming committee, the interrogation group, and the well-meaning mob of his family are about to lay siege on my senses.

The house is loud, not in volume—well it probably is that too—but I'm talking physical appearance. It makes no sense for its location in the quiet woodsy neighborhood. Hanging on an enormous flagpole that towers above the house, is an Italian flag and, just below it, an American one. The door is red, but not a subtle red, a blazing one. There is no sign of a single piece of southern style. No decorative wagon wheels or cute little signs with old-fashioned sayings. The house looks more like it was dropped in here from some northern city.

"Just remember, they can smell fear," Click whispers. "If you cry they will never respect you again. So if you feel yourself on the verge, just run to the bathroom. They'll probably still know, but at least you can save face."

"Wait, why would I cry?" I demand, but Click is already stepping out of the car and coming around to open my door. I'm searching his face as he approaches, looking to see if his lips are curling into a playful smile. But there isn't one. He's either trying hard to play a joke on me, or I'm screwed.

As we walk to the front door I already hear what sounds like a herd of arguing elephants charging toward us. There is laughter and shouting permeating the walls and floating onto the porch where we're standing. I'm sweating, literally dripping sweat all down my back, and I wonder if anyone will notice.

"Click, I don't know if I can do this." I clutch his bicep, digging my nails in and trying to steady myself.

"It's too late now." He shrugs, cupping his hand to his ear, listening to everyone approach. "They've spotted us."

When the door flies open I'm face to face with a sea of children ranging from wobbly toddlers to waist-high and wide-eyed preschoolers. Suddenly, like the Red Sea, they all part obediently to let a short, wide, round-faced woman charge forward.

"My baby," she shrieks as she throws her arms around Click's waist and plants her head on his chest. After a tight hug she yanks him downward with her hands on his cheeks and plants red lipstick kisses all over his face. "I'm so glad you're home."

Up to this point she hasn't noticed me. Which, judging by the aggressive kisses, relieves me. I don't want any of those. Her world looks like it has shrunken down and closed in around her and her baby boy. After a few moments she steps back and takes us both in.

"All things holy, boy, I didn't believe you were really bringing a girl with you. I didn't even set an extra plate."

"It's nice to meet you Mrs. Coglinaese," I say, extending my hand and silently celebrating that I nailed the tough pronunciation of their last name.

"What are you, a businessman or something?" she snipes, looking down at my extended hand as though I'm offering her a moldy tuna sandwich rather than a handshake.

"Um, sorry." I drop my hand and try not to look baffled that I'm apologizing for attempting a socially acceptable and very common form of greeting.

"Call me Corinne. Mrs. Coglinaese was my husband's mother and I hated her." She waves at us to hurry up. "Come on in and get settled. Where are your bags?"

"We're not staying here, Ma. We'll check into a hotel after we visit for a bit," Click asserts, and I brace myself for the backlash he warned me to expect.

"A hotel. What are people going to think? My house isn't good enough for you anymore? People are going to talk." Corinne is waving her hands animatedly as she tries to make her point. I take notice as the children start to scatter like animals sensing an approaching storm.

"The only people who talk about other people's business all live in this house. I think we'll be fine," Click snaps back.

Corinne's eyebrows knit together as she lets out a low and disapproving hum. "You'll eat here, right? My food is still good enough for you, isn't it?"

"Ma, your food is still the best on the planet," Click assures her as he pulls his mother in for another hug, and she seems to relax slightly.

"Yes, it smells delicious in here," I say, trying to navigate my way through compliments.

"Do you eat?" Corinne looks me over slowly, her eyes running from the tips of my shoes to the top of my head.

"Do I eat what?" I ask, thinking there must be more to that question.

"Anything, do you ever eat? You're built like one of those Hollywood people with the eating disorders. You don't throw up your food do you? Because the braciole I made are very expensive and I don't want to waste them on someone who won't enjoy them."

"Corinne," a man says as he steps into the entryway with us. I'm grateful for the distraction, considering I am speechless. The man and Click share many features, though he's thinner than Click and the lines in his weathered face are much deeper. A gorgeous golden retriever with the sweetest disposition follows him. "Leave the poor girl alone. You sound like my mother used to sound when she was talking to you."

At that, Corinne's mouth clamps shut and she seems to be rendered speechless, as I am. A miracle. "I'm Vitty. Please excuse my wife; you've captured the heart of her baby boy, and she's trying to mark her territory."

"It's nice to meet you." We share a quick and knowing smile that shows my appreciation for his intervention. I start to extend my hand and then pull it back quickly, remembering handshakes aren't appropriate for some reason. "I actually love Italian food. I spent some time in Italy when I was younger."

"Well then, we'll have lots to talk about over dinner," Vitty says, clapping his hands together as though everything is working out perfectly, though it certainly doesn't feel that way to me.

"Dad why do you still have that dog? You're allergic. I don't understand why in the world you got it in the first place," Click says, and I'm taken back by the sharp edge of his usually very kind voice.

"Her name is Hemi," Vitty says defensively. "I take a pill every day and it helps with the allergies." He simultaneously scratches the dog behind the ear and rubs his red eyes with the other hand.

Three women, clearly Corinne's daughters, step out from around the corner. They are thinner and slightly taller versions of her, but the way they look at me is identical to the way she does.

"Hello," one says as she plasters a transparent fake smile on her face. "I'm Gabby. It's nice to meet you, Jordan. And so good to have my brother back home, *finally*." She pulls Click in for a hug and I read his face: annoyed.

"Hey Gabby," Click replies, kissing his sister's cheek. "Hey, Tavia, Lona." He pulls his other sisters in. "Where are Tommy, Mick, and Joey?"

"They're all working tonight. They'll see you guys tomorrow night for dinner instead," Tavia says through the tight lips on her pinched expression.

I take note that another large family dinner is already scheduled for tomorrow. Apparently it's implied.

"And Bianca? Should I assume she's the reason I'm back? It would have been easier if you'd told me what was going on over the phone." I can see Click rushing to the point. He really doesn't want to stay here.

10

"We didn't want to risk you getting too busy and not showing up," Lona snipes as her eyebrows rise up nearly to her hairline.

"Yes," Vitty says, lowering his voice slightly. "It's Bianca. She's up in Chucksville . . . dancing. She won't listen to reason."

"Dancing?" Click asks, looking perplexed. "That's what she's always done. Good for her. She's a great dancer."

"Not dancing," his mother cuts in, spinning like a ballerina. "*Dancing*," she reiterates as she moves her body in a provocative way I wish I could unsee.

"Huh?" I can tell Click doesn't get it, and I feel terrible he's about to hear news that I'm sure is going to infuriate him.

I lean in and whisper, "I think she's a stripper." I pray I didn't misread the clues they were giving, because it'll be hard to come back from that error. But I see Corinne nod and hang her head in sorrow.

"What? No she isn't. She'd never do that. Jonah wouldn't allow that for a second. Who told you she was stripping?" Click's words come quick and full of disbelief.

"Dale from the hardware store saw her and came to let me know. Jonah left her. Just up and left her with nothing but the kids and the house. Not an ounce of savings. We had her over for dinner to confront her about the dancing and she lost it. Hasn't been back since. I'm worried about her and the girls," Vitty says, wringing his hands together nervously.

"She's moved out of the house and into an apartment up in Chucksville so she can be closer to that awful place where she works. We've offered to let her and the kids move in here, but she's not interested. Stubborn brat. Another one who's too good for this house," Corinne says, adjusting a doily on the table next to her as she mumbles something in Italian.

"Why did Jonah leave her? Was it because she was stripping?" Click asks as the blood rushes to his frustrated face.

"No, she started dancing after he left. She says she needs the money," Tavia chimes in with snarkiness in her voice. "But I'd sure as hell find another way if it were me. Disgraceful."

Click rubs his temple as though this might help him process the information. "That doesn't make any sense. Bianca and Jonah have been together since high school. He's a part of this family. He already made it through the damn fire of getting accepted by all of you, why would he bail on her?"

"No one knows. She wouldn't say," Gabby hums out as she heads into the dining room, and we all follow. "Let's not talk about it anymore right now." She gestures over to the kids.

"Yes, there will be time to sort it out after we eat," Corinne commands with a wave of her hand. "Jordan, tell us more about yourself. Do you work? All women seem to work now. Sitting home and raising kids isn't good enough for this generation anymore." Corinne shakes her head disapprovingly as she serves heaping piles of grilled asparagus onto everyone's plates.

"I used to be a project manager for a very large investment firm in New York City but I've recently left." I leave out that I was fired. "I'm leaving my options open for a little while. I might do some traveling."

"And a last name like Garcia?" Corinne continues, eying me again. "Your people are Spanish?"

"I . . ." Hesitating, I wonder what story I should tell. I swore when I left Clover I'd start living my authentic life, being who I really am, and discovering what I truly love. But maybe this isn't exactly the best time to test the waters.

"Garcia is a name her family took on when they came to the United States. Her father was an activist for women's rights, and because of the danger that comes with that, Jordan, her mother, and sister fled Afghanistan. Her sister lost her leg in a blast over there, and, not long after they arrived in the United States, her father was killed in Afghanistan."

"What were Spanish people doing in Afghanistan?" Corinne asks as she halts the serving process and waits for much needed clarification.

"She's not Spanish, Ma, she's Afghani. When her family arrived in the United States, for protection, her father insisted they change their name and hide their heritage. But I don't see a reason why she'd need to hide it here." Click's words are a warning even I can decipher. He was telling his family they'd better not challenge this news with any ignorant statements.

"I don't think I understand," Corinne murmurs, bracing herself on the back of her husband's chair, looking as though she might take a spill. "You have people back there, where my baby has been fighting? They could be the ones blowing things up for all we know."

"My family was never associated with terrorism or extremism of any kind," I say flatly, though I do have the urge to jab my fork into Click's leg for putting me in this position. "Most people there do not want violence, they want peace."

"It seems odd if you're not ashamed that you would lie about your name," Corinne accuses as she begins serving everyone again, slapping the food a little harder onto the plates.

"Sometimes we do things to honor our parents wishes even if we don't understand or agree with them. I've never been ashamed of my culture or my country. But my father loved us so deeply that he wanted us to be safe. And so I've done as he asked." I'm not a stupid girl. Lesson one in sales and acquisitions is to know your audience. What do they respect and hold dear? If there would be anything to soften Corinne it would be exploiting her understanding of a parent's desire to protect above all else.

"Hmm," Corinne hums as she loosens her grip on the serving spoon, "I swear you kids don't understand what it's like until you have some of your own. The lengths we'll go to for you, it's impossible to describe. Speaking of which, do you see yourself having a big family? You don't have the hips for it, but once you pop one or two out, the hips just stay wide for the next four or so."

The feminist in me wants to rattle off the hundred reasons this conversation is offensive, but instead I bite my tongue and lift my plate to receive the food she's offering. "I do love kids." I smile, and I can hear Click let out a small grunting laugh. He will pay for this.

Chapter Two

<u>Click</u>

"You did really well," I assure Jordan as I open her car door, kissing her cheek when she passes. I know she's pissed but I don't let that rattle me.

"Is that a joke? Because I thought that was pretty disastrous. Your mother hates me. So do your sisters."

"The only reason you think that is because you've never seen what it looks like when my mom *actually* hates someone. If you had, you'd be celebrating right now. She didn't throw a single thing at you. She didn't curse at you in Italian under her breath. You handled yourself perfectly, just the right amount of restraint and resistance. It's a difficult technique, but you nailed it."

"You talk about her like she's a dictator of a small country."

"What's scary is, if she wanted to be she probably could." I put the car in gear and can't help but laugh at all the faces pressed against the windows watching us pull out of the driveway. "Are you tired or do you have one more adventure in you?" I ask as I tap my fingers against the steering wheel to the beat of the song on the radio.

"What did you have in mind?" Jordan leans over the center console and runs her long, sexy fingernails across my neck and up the back of my head, instantly sending heat through my body. Whatever I was thinking has evaporated for a moment while I mentally run through all the things I'd like to do to Jordan and her perfect body.

"Not that kind of an adventure. Though I can't wait to get to the hotel and rip the buttons off that sweater." I run my hand from her knee up her thigh and land on the

15

heat between her legs. As I move my fingers tantalizingly for a moment I feel her hand tighten around the collar of my shirt, and a small moan passes over her delicate lips.Remembering what brought us to Tennessee in the first place, and the fact that I don't want to stay here long, I reluctantly stop my fingers. "I'm driving out to Chucksville to see Bianca. I don't believe for a second that Jonah just left her and the kids. He wouldn't do that. Something else must be going on and, let me tell you, if she's stripping . . ." I close my fingers tight over the steering wheel and every ounce of filthy thoughts I had about Jordan are gone. All I can think of is what my sister has been doing and why the hell she might be doing it.

"You never really know what's going on in someone else's relationship. Even if you think he's a good guy it doesn't mean—"

"You don't know Jonah. He's been there for me in ways no one else has. When my family is crazy, he's always the one trying to smooth things over. When I was a kid, he and Bianca were dating, and if I had trouble with someone at school he'd come and stick up for me. When I was going to enlist and didn't know how to tell my parents, I told him first, and he came with me to tell them. My other sisters' husbands are okay guys, but I've been deployed for most of their time in our family. Jonah's different. He's like my brother. He's amazing to his daughters. He's never too busy to spend time with them. He throws on a tiara and has a tea party without any hesitation. He's the kind of guy I've always wanted to be like, if I ever had a family of my own. So I'm not jumping to conclusions."

"That sounds a lot like how you were with Adeline in Clover."

"That's because I've always looked up to Jonah. He's a great guy and I'd be lucky if someday I'm half the dad he is."

"Fair enough. What do you plan to do when you find Bianca?" Jordan asks, and I can already see she's not going to agree with my tactics.

"I'm going to go to the strip club and, if she's there, I'm going to drag her ass out and force her to tell me what's really going on."

"Wait, she's older than you, right? She must be in her late twenties. She's not some child being exploited. She's an adult and she's doing what she needs to in order to take care of her family." I can tell any sexy thoughts in Jordan's mind are gone now, too. The fire in her core, where she channels her convictions, has come to life.

"She's my sister and she's taking her clothes off for strangers. You can give me any spin on that story, give it as much women's lib as you'd like, but there is literally nothing that is going to stop me from acting like her brother." Much to my surprise Jordan's lips purse as she nods her head, indicating she won't argue with me. That's a first.

"I can understand that," Jordan croaks out, clearly trying not to shoot back the rebuttal I know she's already crafted.

The rest of the ride is quiet, not awkwardly and uncomfortably silent, just peaceful. My mind is spinning with the intricate lecture I'm compiling for Bianca. I'm guessing Jordan is still processing the emotional attack she just endured at my parents' house. She really did handle it remarkably well for someone who normally doesn't take shit from anyone.

"This is it," I growl out, as though the actual strip club has taken my sister captive and forced her into dancing for money. I'm angry at the painted brick walls and the rusted metal front door. As far as I'm concerned, every car in this parking lot is the vessel of a vile pervert who, if it comes down to it, I will beat down.

"The Apple's Bottom. Classy. Looks like a busy night here," Jordan chirps as she follows my gaze across the parking lot, taking inventory of how many people I might need to beat the hell out of.

"Bunch of losers," I hiss as I pull my car into the only open parking spot, doing so too quickly and sending Jordan's hand to the door, bracing for impact.

"Don't tell me this is your first time in a strip club, because it will change my opinion of you for quite a few reasons." Jordan is trying to remind me that I might not like my sister being in there, but odds are I've been in the audience of one of these establishments at some point too.

"I've been in the military for the last six years; I've seen my share of strip clubs. But there are usually two types of guys in there: guys like me who are with a crowd just because it's the thing to do, and guys who are trolling for girls. They're delusional enough to think the dancers are actually interested in them. They start grabbing and pawing at the girls and usually get tossed out." My hands clench the steering wheel and my knuckles go white from my tight grip.

"If you go in there like this, you'll kill someone," Jordan whispers, and the softness in her voice is so out of character it's enough for me to agree with her. I know it's not easy for her to control her gut reaction and temper, so when she does, I take notice.

"You're right, but why does that seem worth it right now?" I grab the handle and let my fingers hesitate for a moment as her hand reaches across and rests gently on my shoulder.

"I'll go in and see if she's working tonight. If she is I'll find out when her shift is over. There is no point in being here if she isn't even working."

I feel the vice that's clamping down on my chest spin a few notches tighter at the thought of Jordan going in that place. "No way, you're not going in there."

"I think you might be overreacting a little. It's not a cult that brainwashes people. I would say there is zero percent chance they'll recruit me to hop on stage."

"You could be a stripper. You look great naked and you're out of work. I just don't want you going in there and thinking it's glamorous." She pinches the meat on the back of my arm and twists it firmly. I know what I'm saying is stupid, but I'm not feeling very rational right now.

"I am perfectly qualified to be a stripper, and it is well within my right to choose to be one. But I also am not some starry-eyed teenager looking for a good way to pay her way through college. I think I can step through those doors and not be seduced by the smell of sweat and the shine of glitter. I am a grown woman who is quite capable of handling herself." The snap is back in Jordan's voice, and I'm actually glad to hear it. I know that's her true self, and I don't ever want her to feel like she has to hide that from me.

"Get in there and right back out. If you're gone for more than five minutes I'm going to be inside, punching the first couple guys I see." I wish this were an exaggeration, but my fists are clenched and my adrenaline is pulsing fiercely.

"I'll be right back," Jordan assures me as she brushes her fingers across my cheek and loops a finger down my neck to my chest. She pokes it firmly, digging her nail into my muscle. "And you better be sitting right here behaving yourself. Like you said, I'm out of a job, I can't go wasting my money on bail."

Watching her disappear into the club makes my already elevated blood pressure ratchet up even higher. I'm taking her five-minute window very literally as my eyes dart between the watch on my wrist and the door. After the three-minute mark, as the beads of sweat start trailing down my back, I give in. My girlfriend and my sister are alone in a strip club and I've reached my max. I swing my door open, hop out, and slam it behind me with a smashing thud.

I thunder toward the Apple's Bottom and yank open the door, not caring if it comes off its hinges. I know they shouldn't be, but my hands are balled into fists and my nerves are jumping with the energy that used to overtake my body on late night raids while deployed. I spot Jordan standing on her tiptoes and leaning over the bar to try to hear what the bartender is telling her. The smell of stale beer radiates up from the sticky floor as beams of neon lights slash through the dust in the air. This place is a shithole and that enrages me more. Would I feel better if Bianca were dancing in an upscale gentleman's club? Probably not, but knowing this is where she comes every night makes me feel sick.

"Twenty bucks," a large, dark-skinned man with a shaved head barks at me, his palm out flat to collect my money.

"I'm not a customer," I bite back, stepping by him.

"It ain't amateur night so you ain't dancing. That means if you pass through this door you pay me or you get a one-way ticket to the curb."

"You think you can get me back out that door, try me." My teeth gnash together and I can see the man's lip curl into a smile. This is likely his favorite part of the job. As his hand comes up to grab my shirt collar I clamp down on his wrist and spin it until his knees buckle from the pain.

"Click," I hear Jordan shout, and suddenly her nails are digging into the flesh of my arm. It doesn't hurt enough to make me instantly stop, but the sharp edge of her eyes on my face does the trick. I let the man's arm go and take two steps back.

"What the hell are you doing?" Jordan demands as she shoves me back another step, a fire flaming in her eyes. "Bianca is here. She's just starting her shift, but she's not a dancer. She's just waitressing." Jordan gestures toward the bar where a few of the other cocktail waitresses are standing, waiting to fill their trays with drinks. For some reason looking at their lace outfits that barely cover the essentials doesn't make me feel any better. Jordan's tugging my arm, but I've cemented my feet to this dirty floor.

"She's done," I declare, shaking Jordan off with a harshness I regret, but not letting it distract me. I charge up to the bar and shove two drunken idiots out of my way and start shouting my sister's full name. "Bianca Theresa Marie, get your ass over here and make sure you have some damn clothes on." I'm directing my voice to the door that looks like it leads to the back room.

I know my sister, she's not going to take this invasion lightly, but I don't give a damn. I feel two large hands slam down on my shoulder and I know the bouncers aren't taking my disruption well either.

"Get the hell out," an ape-like man demands as he pulls me backward. I stumble a bit but regain my footing and spin skillfully out from under his grip. As I raise my arms, ready for hand-to-hand combat, I hear my sister's familiar scolding tone behind me.

"You had better have a damn good reason for being here. Someone better be dead, *and I mean really dead*, because if not, I'm going to kill you."

I spin to face the most dangerous person in this place, turning my back on the men who want to throw me out. Bianca is far more frightening than they are. "You're leaving, now," I assert and I'm grateful to see she's wearing a long robe and holding it closed tightly. My worst nightmare would be having to sling her over my shoulder if she wasn't decent. I reach my hand out and grab her arm but instantly feel the two men who I've thoroughly pissed off latch onto me again. One is back on my shoulders and the other is pulling my arm off Bianca.

"Stop," Bianca calls, charging forward and pushing the men off me. She's about to go nuclear, I can see it. I've been mapping the warning signs since I turned ten years old. Both my mother and Bianca have fierce tempers; once they're ignited they're not easily defused. When I was a kid this would be right about the time I'd run for the hills. "Get your hands off him, he's my idiot brother."

"Well he didn't pay the cover, and he's causing shit, so I'm kicking his ass on the way out," the man says, cracking his large hairy knuckles at me.

"Good luck with that, Todd; he's Special Forces. He can kill you before you can beg him not to. But he *is* leaving," Bianca says, tugging my arm as we shove past the two men. We collide with Jordan who's cursing me out in Spanish.

"Just come outside," I plead with Bianca, and we all stumble outside and into the dimly lit parking lot. The door closes behind us, trapping the thumping music and commotion inside.

"I swear I am about to rip your throat out and stomp on it. How dare you come to the place I work and embarrass me like that? I am not a child." Bianca's words are spoken with such emphasis that I can feel my cheeks heating up like a kid being reprimanded. It isn't until I remind myself what this *place of work* is, that I fire back.

"A strip club? Really, Bianca, what the hell are you doing?"

"I told you not to go in there, Click," Jordan snaps, shoving my shoulder back angrily.

"Who the hell are you?" Bianca asks Jordan, and it hits me that these two women have a remarkably similar ability to cut through bullshit and tell you you're an idiot. What I didn't consider is how terribly they may get along.

"I'm Jordan," she explains, folding her arms across her chest. "I'm the person trying to keep him from acting like a complete asshole tonight."

"You're doing a terrible job," Bianca responds, her voice softer, and I'm relieved to see her dial it down slightly.

I take advantage of the moment and try to reason with my sister. "Bianca, tell me what's going on. How did you get *here*?" I ask, my eyes full of disgust as I gesture toward the club. The look that spreads across my sister's face brings me as close to tears as I've been in a long time. I've just wounded her. Badly.

"Don't you dare look at me like I'm trash. How did I get here? You think any of the girls in there are just living it up and having a good time? No, they're here for the same reason I am. Money. I need it. This is how I'm going to get it. So you can get the hell out of here. I don't need you judging me."

"I'm not judging you," I lie, and she can read that instantly. "Can you get in the car with us and get out of here? Let's just go talk. We can figure this out together."

"I know this is hard for you to believe, but you can't fix everything. You can't save everyone. I'm going back in there, and I'm finishing my shift. You are going to your car and leaving. And you," she says pointing at Jordan, "are going to make sure he does. If you still want to talk to me tomorrow I'll text you my new address here in Chucksville, and you can come by. The girls would like to see you; they miss you."

"Where are they now? I can go be with them for you. Are they safe?"

"*Are they safe?*" Bianca parrots back, full of indignation. "Yes, my children are safe right now. Just because I'm serving drinks here doesn't mean I've started neglecting the most important things in my life. The only person who's hurt them is their father. I'm sure you think Jonah can do no wrong but you misjudged him. We all did." Bianca pulls her robe tighter and turns on her heels. I have a thousand questions, a million demands, but as I feel Jordan's hand squeeze my bicep I know there isn't anything else I can say tonight.

"We'll go see her tomorrow," Jordan whispers and I hang my head, feeling at first sad and then filling again with anger.

I get back in the car, this time not thinking to open Jordan's door for her, but she doesn't seem to mind. She's quiet, and I know that isn't an easy thing for her.

"Don't you want to tell me I was wrong? Isn't this your cue to tell me I screwed up?" I feel the urge to argue with her as if it might bring me some release but she's too smart for that.

"We'll go see her tomorrow," she repeats as she pulls her hair up into a ponytail and buckles her seatbelt. "It'll all work out."

Even though I know I shouldn't let my thoughts go there, my mind reels with the idea that my sister has just walked back into that strip club. My anger hasn't subsided, my emotions are still rubbed raw, but I have no choice but to put the car in reverse and leave her here. As much as I hate it, Bianca is right. For a long time I've been learning this lesson the hard way. I can't save everyone. That's becoming abundantly clear.

Chapter Three

<u>Jordan</u>

I'm depressed that this is the first time in my adult life I've cared enough about someone to hurt when they hurt. It's like late onset empathy. How did I live so long being so selfish? Watching the tumultuous conflict raging inside Click tonight has my heart aching for him. I've painted myself the ultimate problem solver in business, but in matters of family I'm clueless.

His rhythmic breathing next to me in bed is not one of sleep. It's one of restlessness while staring at the ceiling. I know because I'm doing the same thing. We've been checked into the hotel a couple miles from the Apple's Bottom for nearly two hours but neither of us can sleep. Every time I consider speaking, I realize I have nothing productive to say.

So instead, when all words and sleep escape me, I roll toward him and press my body to his side. He lifts his arm and welcomes me below it, tucking me in tightly. I brush my hand across his bare chest, looking for the perfect spot to rest it.

"You're heart is racing," I whisper, and even in a hushed voice it cuts through the silent room.

"I'm so pissed." He exhales as he covers my hand with his. "I still want to go back there and beat the hell out of every single person. I don't even want to tell you what was going through my head tonight. The things I wanted to do, they aren't good."

"I think it's justified, considering the situation," I try to reason, but I have a feeling he's not just talking about tonight.

"There are moments I feel like I'm back in the war. I forget I'm not in the desert anymore. I sometimes have a hard time separating that. It bothers me."

His words come reluctantly. It's easy to tell he doesn't want to have this conversation, but I think he knows he needs to. There were signs in Clover that the time he spent in a warzone had him carrying an extra burden.

"Have you talked to anyone? There must be resources for you when you come home, right?" I actually have no clue what I'm talking about. I've had a pretty steadfastly stubborn view about the military and war over the years, so I haven't really concerned myself with the support system provided for returning soldiers. The buzzwords are all over television and in the news. I know there's an epidemic of post-traumatic stress out there, but damn if I know what you're supposed to do to help.

"I'm fine," he says, patting my hand. "Things get bad, and then they get better. It's not something I can explain or talk about. I'm not sure you'd understand."

"I wouldn't," I admit, feeling like being honest is the only option I have. "I don't think people can understand what it's like over there if they haven't been through it. I'm always here to listen, but I'm not going to pretend that I'll say the right thing. I probably won't."

"It's not really about saying anything," Click explains as his arm closes in tighter around me. "Sometimes I just need to feel *here*, instead of still over *there*. Do you know what I mean?"

"No," I confess, angry with myself for my ignorance.

"I need to be rooted in something. I need to feel connected because over there that didn't happen. Survival was about being disconnected. Physically and emotionally. But with you, touching you and loving you—it reminds me that that part of my life is over and this part is my reality." His hand lifts and comes to my cheek, brushing it lightly. His fingers swirl in a circular motion, moving slowly toward my mouth. I feel his thumb brush across my lips and I meet it with a kiss. In an instant, I've gone from not knowing what he needs, to knowing exactly what he's telling me. He wants to feel. Because feeling reminds him of being here, and if he's here, he isn't still over there.

As he strums his thumb again over my lips I part them and he pushes it into my mouth. I swirl my tongue around it, eliciting a moan from him. I release his thumb from my lips and bring my body on top of him. I strain in the dim light to read his face, cautiously trying to make sure I haven't misread the situation. For the first time tonight the veins in his neck aren't pulsing and his jaw is finally relaxed. *This is what he wants.*

I pull my long hair to the side and twist it back over my shoulder to keep it out of my face. His hands are gripping my hips tightly then sliding up my ribs and back down again. Slipping my shirt over my head, I feel his hands clamp down on my hard nipples, drawn there like magnets. The pinch and pull is enough to soak my panties as I grind myself against his firmness. Pleasure has never been so easy to attain. A few hard strokes against him and I could easily be shuddering. But I don't. I pull back and slip off my wet panties, all I had on with my T-shirt. He works his way out of his shorts, and I see his firmness spring up, ready for me.

I lean down and press my full body against him, kissing him with a passion that feels as much like home to me as I hope it does to him. His hands get twisted up in my hair and I love the tug and force he handles me with tonight. There is urgency in his movements. He doesn't just want me, he needs me, and every move proves it. It's different and unfamiliar but it's actually heightening my excitement.

Rather than let me ride him, he quickly scoops up my legs and shifts himself upright. In a quick and dominant motion he's on his feet and I'm in his arms. My legs grip around him, his hardness still rubbing against me as he drops me down on the desk in the corner of the hotel room. Though it's cool beneath my skin, the heat we're creating keeps me from caring. I shove everything below my hands off the desk and let it crash to the floor. He parts my legs, unapologetically pushing them open. Gripping my hair tightly between his fingers he tips my head back and his mouth devours my neck as he plunges inside me. I gasp at the force of it, but clutch my legs around him tightly before he can back out. His piercing depth is a mix of pain and pleasure, and I don't want to let go.

I want to elicit the same feeling in him. As he thrusts deeper and deeper into me I lean forward and bite hard on the flesh between his shoulder and his neck, making him tug even more at the handful of my hair he's still grasping.

Click is grunting as he moves at a frantic pace. He pushes my legs even wider and yanks me closer to the edge of the desk. The new position has me so close to ecstasy I start chanting his name. Reading my readiness, his hand releases my hair and cups my breast, pinching my nipple as I cry out in pain, but I hold his hand in place, begging him not to stop. As my body tightens around him, I shudder and let my nails drag deep into the skin of his back as I ride out the wave of pleasure he's given me.

My body relaxes and he scoops me up again and spins me toward the bed. I'm on my back catching my breath as he plunges back inside me, and stares into my face. After a few deep hard strokes I feel him come, his hand on my shoulder, bearing down on my body and taking every last ounce of pleasure he can. I'm thrilled to be able to give it to him. If he's forgotten the conflict raging inside him for even a few minutes, I feel like I've accomplished something.

Chapter Four

Click

Whatever stress and anxiety Jordan lifted from me last night has crept its way back in. I'm knocking on the faded beige door of the address Bianca texted me, and I still have no clue what I'm going to say to her. Everything I talked out with Jordan on the ride over, she vetoed. No, I could not tell her she was raised better than this. No, I could not accuse her of losing her mind or just wanting attention. And most importantly, I could not tell her that she had to quit. Jordan told me everything I couldn't say but she stopped shy of telling me what might actually work.

My sister huffs loudly as she pulls open the door barely enough for her head to stick out. "I told you to come over today, not first thing in the morning."

"Are you letting us in?" I ask, meeting her attitude tit for tat.

Without a word she swings the door wide open and rudely walks away, back into her tiny apartment. She bends down and grabs a handful of toys then a single sock on her way to the living room.

A thundering herd of tiny feet comes racing around the corner, and before I can blink there are two little nightgown-clad girls jumping into my arms. The sweet smell of shampoo reminds me how much I love them. They both favor Jonah; they inherited his sandy colored hair and slightly too big ears. But they have Bianca's smile, even though I haven't yet seen hers on this trip.

"Girls," I chuckle and pretend they are choking me, "you're so big I can barely hold you up."

"Daphne and Penny, go clean up those toys in your room; I'm not going to tell you again. You can come play with your uncle when that's done." I see a stern and tired scowl press across my sister's face and I know she's at her wits' end. As the girls scurry away into the other room, Bianca gestures toward the plaid out-of-date couch, and Jordan and I take a seat.

"I'm not interested in a lecture, so save your breath if that's what you're here for." Bianca doesn't sit. Instead, she folds her arms across her chest and cocks a goading eyebrow at me, daring me to say something stupid.

"Where is Jonah?" I try to keep my question direct and free of the overwhelming emotions I feel.

"Damned if I know. A month ago he comes home from work and tells me he's leaving. He gives me the house and the kids and drains our savings account. Literally doesn't say a word to me as he grabs a bag of his clothes and leaves. That's it. One day everything is fine, the next my life is over. My best friend leaves me without a single explanation."

"That doesn't make any sense. He would never just abandon the girls like that. Has he even called? Have you tried to find him?"

"Why would I try to find him? He's a bastard for what he's done. I never want to see him again."

"You should have called me." I try to deliver my words without the daggers of blame, but it seems impossible.

"Don't act like you're all about putting family first. We've come second to the Marines for over six years."

"I was deployed, Bianca. That was different than now. I couldn't just leave my post every time one of the

32

kids had a play at school or a birthday party. I had a job to do."

"Hey, I get that signing up made you a brave kid. We were all really proud. What I don't get is, after that place nearly killed you a dozen times, after it ruined some of the best parts of you, why you would go back. How could you choose to go back there when your family wanted you home? You did your four years. You should have been done."

"Hold on," Jordan demands, her eyes wide and full of fire. I have my own answer to Bianca's question. It revolves around not ever wanting to leave my buddies out on that battleground without me. But before I can make that case Jordan is speaking at a rapid fire pace.

"How could he reenlist? That's your question? You think he did that because he didn't care about his family, because he wanted to be away?"

"You don't understand," Bianca bites back, her tone as steely as Jordan's.

"No, I don't think you understand because you've been living in this country your whole life and it's made you complacent. You can send those girls to school, they can learn to read and write. They can wear the clothes they choose and listen to the music they like. Last night I was in your corner when it came to defending your choice of profession because you have the right to do it if you want. Know that, in other parts of the world, showing even a few inches of your ankle could have had you dragged into the street and stoned. So when you sit there and question your brother's loyalty to your family, realize his sacrifice for his country is the reason you have the freedoms you do today."

Jordan's fierce reaction to Bianca's cutting words sends a lump to my throat. It wasn't that long ago she herself questioned my motives for being a Marine. Now here she was defending my honor.

"I'm sorry. I'm under a lot of stress and I'm taking that out on you." Bianca sighs and slumps into the chair across from us. "I am grateful for everything you've done, Click. I'm in awe of you really. But I've got this under control. You can go back to Mom and Dad and tell them to back off. Then you can take off to wherever else in the world you'd rather be than here."

She's right. I could lie and try to convince her that being back in Tennessee is nostalgic and heartwarming, but really I would suffocate here.

"Why didn't you just move back with Mom and Dad? You know they'd have helped you." I deflected the subject from my own problems.

Bianca huffs out an annoyed laugh. "Isn't that ironic coming from you? If you want answers from me, try opening up yourself. You were home for just over a day after your last tour and then you were gone. You were finally free and took off. Why was that?" The arrogant smile on her face tells me she already knows the answer but doesn't intend to let me off the hook.

"Mom is too much for me sometimes," I admit. "She's always digging for more and more information about things I don't want to talk about. She wants answers I don't have. Dad, well, he's just been completely weird. He acts like I wasn't gone at all. What's up with the dog, why does he have a dog now?" I scratch at my head as I contemplate my parents' strange behavior. "You know what makes me most mad about the dog?" I ask and instantly see Bianca light with recognition.

"I knew that was going to bother you," she interjects and I see Jordan looks confused.

"What? Why does your dad having a dog bother you so much?" Jordan asks, looking back and forth between the two of us.

"It's our hostage word. And it has been for the last six years. Now I have to come up with something else."

"What the hell is a hostage word?" Jordan twists her face up in confusion.

"If we were ever in distress or taken hostage and we were communicating with each other we were supposed to mention something about a dog. Like, *Did you feed the dog?* or *Don't forget to walk the dog*," Bianca explains.

"Right. And now every time I hear dad talk about the damn dog I think he's in some kind of distress. I have to come up with a whole new distress word." I don't hide my frustration. It's likely a stupid reason in most people's eyes to be mad but I can't help it.

"It's a good dog," Bianca says in a softer voice and then seems to remember what we were talking about before we got off track. "I'm not letting you off the hook so easily. Our situations aren't that different."

Knowing I owe her an answer, I continue, "I don't have things sorted in my own head yet, so I can't be there with everyone wanting more from me."

"Exactly," Bianca shoots back. "I don't want to sit around the dinner table and speculate where Jonah is. I don't need Mom implying if I were a better cook maybe he'd still be around. I don't want Dad acting like Jonah never existed either. You have your reasons for not being there, and I have mine."

"I can come up with some money." I turn my eyes to the ground, knowing she's going to hate my offer but that won't keep me from making it.

"You can't come up with the amount of money I need. I have a plan. I'm staying here through the summer. Six months. I can swing the rent on this dive apartment and save up a year's worth of mortgage payments for the house. This place is much closer to work for me. I can't be over an hour and a half from the house every night. That's why I rented this dump. By the time Daphne is ready for kindergarten in September we'll be back in our house. I can give my daughters the life I had planned for them before Jonah betrayed us. Even if you could give me the money, I wouldn't take it."

"Why? I know you're stubborn, but why are you digging in on this?"

"When someone screws you over," Jordan chimes in as she locks eyes with Bianca, "the last thing you want to do is become beholden to someone else."

"I'm her brother," I shoot back, annoyed that Jordan is trying to make Bianca's case for her.

"He was my husband," Bianca whispers with the first sign of sadness on her face, replacing the anger. "He was the other half of my life, my future. And one day, without any explanation, he destroyed that. There is no way I'm ever giving that kind of power to anyone else ever again. If I can't get something by myself then I won't get it. I have a plan and it's going to work as long as you stop showing up at my job."

"How am I supposed to let you do this? I can't just walk away today and leave you like this."

"It's hilarious to me that you don't understand how long we all had to do that for you. Do you think it was

36

easy worrying that every time the phone rang it would be news about something happening to you? Loving people isn't about controlling them and forcing them to live a life that doesn't make you worry. If you love me then the only thing I need you to do is run interference with Mom and Dad. Tell them I'm doing all right and not to worry."

"They'll still worry."

"I know that, but if they hear it from you it will buy me some time. That's all I'm asking."

I turn from Bianca's pleading eyes to Jordan's empathetic ones. "Fine," I resign reluctantly. "But I'm keeping tabs on you, and if anything gets out of control at that place you call me."

"Fine. I will. Do you want to spend some time with the girls before you leave?" Bianca asks, looking like I've lifted an anvil off her shoulders.

"I'll come back tomorrow and visit with them. I've got some stuff to take care of today."

"Tomorrow, huh? So you're not getting the hell out of here as fast as you can?"

"I'll be in Tennessee for a while." I can't help but catch Jordan's shocked eyes as I stand and start heading for the door. This isn't what I've been saying all along, but now leaving doesn't seem like an option any more. Not until this is settled.

Chapter Five

<u>Click</u>

"You did really well," Jordan says, leaning across the center console of the car and kissing my cheek. "It's not easy to sit back and watch someone you love make a choice you disagree with, but I think it's admirable that you handled it so well."

"Like hell," I murmur as I dig my phone out of my pocket and start dialing.

"Who are you calling?"

"Luke. He's the only one who can help straighten this shit out."

"Are you going to ask him for money? She won't take it. She needs to do this on her own; you heard her."

"I'm not asking for money," I retort flatly and then press the phone to my ear, which silences Jordan. "Luke, it's Click. Sorry to bother you but I need a favor."

I've only known Luke for a short time, but he's a solid and reliable friend, and it's good to hear his voice. Being in Clover, North Carolina, was a blessing for me, and Luke is a big part of that.

"Hey man, how's it going in Tennessee? Did you get to the bottom of whatever kind of trouble your sister is in?"

"Yeah, her husband left her suddenly and she's serving drinks at a strip club to try to make ends meet." Saying it out loud to someone turns my stomach to cement.

"Holy shit, dude. That *is* bad. How can I help?"

"I need to find her husband. I know you have contacts everywhere. Could one of them give me a hand in tracking him down?"

"Yes, unless it will make me an accessory to murder. Do you plan on leaving this guy breathing or not?"

"I just want to talk to him. Something isn't right. He's not the kind of guy to just bail on his family. Something must have happened. My sister isn't interested in accepting a loan from me and she's dead set on trying to get her life back even if it means she's got to—"

"Text me his information and I'll see if I can get any leads for you," Luke interrupts, saving me from having to rehash what Bianca is doing.

"Thanks, hey how is everything in Clover? Devin, Rebecca, and Adeline okay?"

"Things are expanding quickly here. It's keeping us pretty busy but that's a good thing. We could certainly use you and Jordan back here. Do you think that's in the cards?"

"Could be. I honestly can't think past today right now, but once I get things sorted out here, we'll be hitting the road. I guess we could end up back in Clover."

"That's my vote if I get one. I'll let you know what I come up with on your brother-in-law. Try to keep your cool out there."

"I'll try," I assure him half-heartedly as I hang up the phone. Jordan's eyes are running up and down my face. I suck in a deep breath before I turn my gaze toward her.

"Really?" she asks as she shakes her head in disappointment. "You think hunting down Jonah is going to fix any of this? She doesn't ever want to see him again."

"You've never met him. I've known Jonah since I was twelve years old. He's been in love with my sister for sixteen years. He loves his daughters. I consider him a brother. There has to be more to the story, and if I can't get Bianca to take my help then maybe getting answers from Jonah is the best I can do."

"You're meddling in things when she very clearly just asked you not to. Odds are you're going to end up looking like the bad guy no matter what the outcome is."

"I can handle that if it means getting Bianca back to a normal life."

"And you plan on staying in Tennessee while you work it all out? You sure you can handle that? I heard you last night. You were having a nightmare. It sounded intense. I think being back here is really bothering you."

I feel a rush of blood course through my body toward my face at the thought of Jordan glimpsing the shadows that lurk in the dark places of my mind. "I'm fine." I shrug off the conversation and roll down my window, letting the cool air and the rushing sound of the wind take over.

"You can talk to me, you know," Jordan says loudly over the noise I've created. "When we first met I wasn't very empathetic about the military. I still have a lot of problems with war in general, but I can separate that from what it means to fight for your country."

"That's not why I don't want to talk about it. I know you support me and I also know if I needed to talk you'd be there to listen. I feel like I do a pretty good job of fending off most of it. If I start talking about it, I might lose my footing."

"What about talking to a professional, someone who deals with this stuff all the time? I'm sure they are prepared for that type of thing."

"A few nightmares aren't going to ruin my life. My six-year-old nephew has them all the time and he seems to be doing fine."

"I'm guessing his are about dinosaurs and monsters, not smoke and bleeding ear drums."

The fact that her examples come directly from the nightmare I had last night tells me I was talking in my sleep. I don't know exactly how much or what she heard but, either way, it's not what I want. "Can we drop it?"

"Of course, let's get back to talking about overstepping boundaries in your sister's personal life."

"Can we drop that, too?" I plead, making sure my eyes look sad enough to win Jordan over.

"What do you want to talk about?"

"This is going to be your second dinner at my family's house. Now that you've met them it won't be quite as relaxed and friendly as last night."

"That was relaxed?"

"For them it was. Tonight is going to be about sizing you up and trying to find your weaknesses. All three of my sisters' husbands will be there, and they are kind of dopes. Usually nice dopes but challenging."

"Good thing I don't have any weaknesses."

"Yeah, except for the way you argue a point to death, even completely unimportant things. You snore like a grizzly bear. You slurp your coffee. Should I go on?"

"I never pegged you as a liar, Click, but apparently you are. I certainly do not snore or slurp my coffee. Nor do I beat a point to the death. I occasionally, and very intentionally, let you win. I relent when I realize my

41

opponents don't know what the hell they're talking about. See, I'm about to do it right now."

"Just get your game face on," I tease as I grab her knee and tickle it the way that always sends her into a flailing fit.

She slaps my hand away and drops the smile from her face. "All kidding aside, Click, I'm here for you. No matter what, I've got your back."

"We call that having my six," I explain as I glance over and brush her dark bangs away from her eyes then turn back toward the road. "That's the part I miss most about being deployed. It's easy for people to say they have your back, but over there it was true. You watched out for your brother next to you and they did the same. It's the only way to survive. I miss that, but with you I feel like I have a piece of that back. I know you're looking out for me. That you'd do anything for me."

"You miss it over there? I didn't realize that."

I can see the confusion on her face and I start to regret saying anything about it. "I don't miss the war, but I miss my buddies. Some of them are still over there and it kills me not to be with them. Some have been deployed again and again and I'm here enjoying the freedom we all take for granted every day."

Though she tries to disguise it, I can see the fear in her eyes. She wants to ask me more. I'm sure she wants to know exactly what I mean, but the answers might not be what she wants to hear.

"I'll watch your six," she asserts as she reaches across and puts her hand to my cheek. I wish we weren't driving because I'd like to be able to take in the look in her eyes. I truly am grateful to have her loyalty.

Chapter Six

<u>Jordan</u>

"Two days in row, you're about to break your record," Click's brother-in-law, Mick jokes as he slaps him on the shoulder. He's a short, stocky man with a gap-toothed grin, a constant sweaty forehead, and a five o'clock shadow. He's wearing the amount of gold that screams, *Hey I can afford gold, can you?* "I thought for sure you'd have hightailed it out of town again." I see the look of annoyance growing on Click's face. "We're all taking bets."

"Leaving town. There seems to be a lot of that going around," his sister Tavia hisses like she's trying to hide her happiness. Maybe she's not happy about Bianca's trouble but she's enjoying the gossip. "You went to see Bianca, right? What did she say? What really happened with Jonah?" The excitement on her face makes me want to slap the lipstick right off her mouth. I never understand people who take joy in the suffering of others.

"Tavia," Click's mother cuts in, "I told you I would ask him. She's my daughter and I have the right to know what's going on first."

Like vultures hovering over the carcass of Bianca's roadkill of a life, they are all trying to rip off their piece. Maybe Click is accustomed to this, but I'm not.

"She's fine," Click says flatly as he leans against the wall in the den and crosses his arms over his chest. "She doesn't know what happened with Jonah. She's as puzzled as the rest of us."

"Well, I'll tell you one thing, and let this be a lesson to the rest of you girls here," Corinne stares right at me,

43

her finger pointing in my direction, "a man does not leave a woman who can make a lasagna like mine. Next time I'm teaching you something in the kitchen you might want to pay more attention if you care about your marriages."

I let out a small gasp of disbelief as Bianca's premonition about what she would face comes to fruition. All eyes turn toward me and I feel words bubbling at the back of my throat that I know I shouldn't say, but I can't help myself.

"If a man left me because I burnt a lasagna I'd be glad he was gone. I'd hope I'd have more content to my character than just the ability to mix up some ingredients the right way." Eyes go wide and mouths drop open. All but Corinne's. Her face does the opposite. Eyes narrow and lips purse.

"A woman's role is to raise her family. She's on this earth to feed them and teach them things like how to speak with respect around someone else's table." Corinne's face is growing redder by the second.

"Well then I *respectfully* disagree with that statement, and since I don't think we'll find common ground, let's just move on to something else." I don't think anyone is accustomed to this kind of talk. "Tavia, Click tells me you're a beautiful seamstress. I'm a fanatic when it comes to fashion and design. I would love to see some of your work."

"His name is not *Click*," Corinne snaps as she takes two large steps toward me. I should be intimidated but I'm not. Somewhere on the ride over tonight I convinced myself it's ridiculous to act different than I usually do just because Click's family is challenging. If I do plan on being in his life then it won't serve to be someone I'm not. They are either going to love me or hate me; I'm going to give them my authentic self and they can decide.

"Excuse me?" I ask, not sure I heard Corinne correctly through her pursed and angry lips.

"His name is Vittorino. Same as his father. We call him Vit, or V but we don't call him Click. Because that isn't his name."

"I didn't pick it," I argue back. "That's just how he introduced himself to me and what he prefers to be called. So I respect that, and it's what I'll call him."

"Ma," Click says, raising a hand up begging her to stop. "You know that's the name my platoon gave me. We've had this conversation a hundred times. It's my name. It's who I am."

"It's not. Maybe it's who you were over there but you are home now, and it's time for you to start acting normal again."

"Corinne," Click's father says with a warning tone. "Now is not the time. He's home, it's all over, let's let sleeping dogs lie."

"Speaking of dogs," Click says with anger in his voice. "Can we please talk about this dog? Why do you have him? You don't even like dogs."

The oven timer dings loudly from the kitchen and breaks the tension for a moment. "Let's just eat," Corinne breathes out as she hustles toward her food before it burns. Everyone moves to the dining room and takes a seat. The silence is speaking volumes about the level of tension.

Corinne comes out with serving platters of food in each arm and begins circling the table, slapping everything down onto the empty plates. I notice she skips over the women to serve all the men first. It's archaic in my opinion, but to each his – or in this case, her - own.

I turn my attention toward Mick as he begins to ask me a question. "So, Jordan, Tavia tells me you're a Muslim. Don't you have to wear one of those whole body sheets?" I watch in disgust as he uses his thumbnail to pry something from his teeth.

I choke on my drink and try to process his ignorance. "You should know not all Muslims wear burkas. However, I'm not Muslim. I don't practice any religion at the moment. I was born in Afghanistan but have spent the majority of my life in the United States. I'm as American as any of you."

"Well, I think Italian descent versus Arab descent would make us a little more American than you," he replies, adjusting the Italian flag emblem on the pennant around his neck. "Our country isn't blowing things up like a bunch of crazy people."

"No, the road to your heritage is just littered with the bodies of innocent people caught in the cross fire of the mafia. Your history is one full of racketeering, extortion, and intimidation."

"Yeah it is," Mick says as he high-fives Tommy. The pride my intended insult creates only makes me more annoyed.

"Mrs. Chenny called me again today," Corinne interrupts as she takes her seat by her husband. This sounds like an innocuous topic of conversation but judging by Click's visceral reaction, I can tell it has a deeper meaning.

"Really, Ma, you're going there again? I've told you I don't want to talk to her. I didn't know her son, and I don't have anything to tell her."

"I don't understand why you won't talk to her. Though it shouldn't surprise me, since you won't talk to *your own mother* about the last six years of your life. You know how embarrassing it is when people ask me where you were deployed, what you did over there, and I can barely answer them? Do you know how that makes me look?"

"If you were a little less concerned with how you look to everyone maybe you'd realize that it's not something I want to talk about, and I have my reasons."

"Well, poor Mrs. Chenny lost her son over there. He was blown up so badly they couldn't even have an open casket at his funeral. All she wants to do is talk to you about what it was like. She wants to know if you ever met him while he was there. I can't believe you won't even give her that."

"It's not a mixer, Mom. You don't just meet a bunch of people like on a cruise ship. I didn't know him. If I had to bet my life on it, I'm sure I'd find out you called her; she didn't call you. I'm sure you are driving this entire conversation. And there is a damn good chance it's as intrusive and rude to her as it is to me."

Corinne takes the serving spoon from the salad and launches it across the room. While it's not directed at anyone in particular, it still has me jumping. Who the hell does that?

"You don't tell me anything. I don't know anything about what happened to you there. I try to ask and you get mad. That's not fair to me." Corinne's face is blood red and her hand is slamming down on the table as she talks.

"Corinne, maybe there isn't anything to tell. Not every Marine sees action," Click's father says, and I can see what Click means about his father's avoidance of the topic. What a toxic mix his parents must be when they argue about this. One begging to know more, the other pretending it never happened.

Click stands and grabs my hand so I stand as well. "You want to know what the last six years of my life were like?" he asks, and Corinne's face lights up with a hopefulness.

"Yes."

"Somehow, even though it was a warzone, it was quieter than this house. Even though I wasn't related to a single person, they felt more like family to me than any of you right now. I risked my life on a regular basis and I was more relaxed than I am tonight. Bianca is fighting to keep her head above water, and she'd rather drown than come back to this house and deal with this chaos. So if you're worried about anything, worry about that."

Corinne howls like a wounded animal and clutches her chest as though she might die. Click has me by the wrist and we're barreling toward the front door. I don't want him to leave like this, but I also agree with every word that has come out of his mouth. When we step on the porch he slams the door so forcefully the windows rattle.

I'm too shocked to say a word as we fall into the car, he throws it in drive, and we skid down the road.

"I'm so sorry, Click," I whisper, my eyes still wide with disbelief. "I shouldn't have been argumentative. I didn't realize it would turn into that."

"You have nothing to apologize for. It's me who should be apologizing. They were insulting to you, and you deserve better than that. They don't know anything about your culture except what they hear on television.

Spin that against the fact that I was over there and it's twisted itself into something ignorant. So I'm sorry."

"I couldn't care less about that. I'm worried about you. Your mother was very upset. You were completely in the right, but still. I don't want to see this ruin your entire relationship. She's still your mother and—"

"I forget sometimes that not everyone grows up like this. That argument, while not that common for my mother and me, considering I haven't been around much, is still a very normal occurrence around that table. It's either Bianca allowing Daphne to play soccer instead of a *girl* sport, or it's how Tommy won't eat my mother's chicken parmesan because he doesn't like the way she pounds out the chicken. Something gets thrown and someone storms out. It happens, and it happens frequently."

"And then what happens next? How do you work it out?"

"We don't. We show up the next week and passively snipe at each other until the next blowup. That argument replaces the last. It's how they work."

"That sounds awful," I bite my lip as punishment for blurting out something so insensitive. "I mean, that seems like a really hard dynamic to live in."

"It is. My mother wants me to sit down and bare my soul to her. She wants to save me. It's her badge of honor to wear. Before I went to boot camp I was a mama's boy. If my heart was broken I turned to her. But she doesn't understand this is a different kind of heartbreak. It can't be fixed with cannoli and threatening to beat the hell out of the girl who wouldn't go to the snowball dance with me."

49

I hear the word *heartbreak* and bank a clue to what Click is really feeling. He's not transparent about much, so I've been gathering up the little bits and pieces, trying to understand what he's feeling. Heartbreak wasn't on my radar. But I suppose seeing what he's seen would break your heart, I just hadn't thought of it that way.

"What if you just told her a little bit. Just the basics."

"That's like feeding a drop of blood to a shark. She won't stop until she's gotten every last piece of me. I don't have it to give right now."

"What do we do now?" I ask, as Click races down the dirt road leading away from his house.

"We go back to the hotel and wait to hear something from Luke. All I want to do is track Jonah down, get some answers, and put this place in my rearview mirror again. I mean, look at it here—there is nothing. There are only fields and farms. Nosy neighbors with nothing to do. It's exhausting." As Click turns to his left to look over the freshly plowed farm I see a flash of something dart out from the trees on my side of the car. I scream, but it's too late. Even though Click's foot comes down heavy on the brake, we make impact. Hard impact.

Chapter Seven

Click

I reach to my side to get a hold of my weapon but it isn't there. The blast must have sent it airborne. I'm sure I still have my knife strapped to my ankle unless my leg's been blown off. At least if there are insurgents here I should be able to defend myself. But my men—are they hurt? Are they dead? I know I need to fight to stay conscious, to open up my eyes and assess the situation, triage, and radio for medics. No matter what pain my body is enduring, I need to fight through the fog to do my job.

I reach toward my backpack for my radio, but that's gone too. Where are my supplies? I can feel just the material of a cotton T-shirt, not my camo. What's happening? Am I dead?

I crack open my eyes and look down at my hands. They are covered with blood. Fumbling for my seatbelt, I have to exit the vehicle and secure the situation. That's my training. Though the world is spinning around me and thoughts are darting back and forth from the corners of my mind, I will my body to move. I throw my sore shoulder into the door of the Humvee and, as it swings open, I plummet to the ground. I was wrong. My knife isn't on my ankle. I have no weapons. Such vulnerability in a hostile zone fills me with primal adrenaline. I must protect my men until help can arrive. I need to find my radio to call medevac to come get us out of this hostile territory. I start to yell the names of each of my men as I hear a voice over my shoulder.

A man I don't know is there, and with all the strength I can muster, I reach up and yank his body to the ground next to me combat style. He's gasping for air as I wrap an arm around his neck and my legs around his body. If there are more insurgents coming, my only hope will be to arm myself with this man's weapons.

As his body begins to weaken I hear a woman's voice. She's screaming my name. Begging me to stop. Her face has come down to my level and her nose is nearly pressed to mine.

Jordan?

Nothing makes sense as two worlds collide in my mind, and I realize I'm not where I thought I was. This man is not who I thought he was. Nothing is as I believed. I release the man who I now see is dressed in jeans and a flannel shirt. He scurries away from me on his hands and knees, keeping an eye on my movements. He's clearly afraid I could strike again.

Jordan's hands are clamped down on my shoulders as tears streak down her cheeks, cutting a path through the blood flowing from a gash on her forehead. I blink hard, over and over again, trying to focus on where I am. She's still screaming my name, slapping lightly at my cheek.

"I'm okay," I whisper as I regain my grip on the present. "What happened? What did we hit? Are you hurt?"

"A deer, a big one. Like with antlers," Jordan says with a whimper. "It came out of nowhere and we hit it. What happened to you? Why were you strangling that guy?" Her eyes are wild with a storm of concern.

"I'm sorry," I say to her and then to the man who still looks terrified. "I'm sorry. I didn't know where I was for a minute. I was somewhere else."

He nods his head, but I can tell he doesn't understand. He doesn't know what I mean. But I focus back on Jordan. "You're cut." I reach out and touch Jordan's forehead but she pushes my hand away.

"So are you. I think your nose is broken. You hit your head. We need to get to a hospital."

"I've already called; they should be here any minute," the frightened man says as he gets back on his feet and moves a few steps away from us. "The buck is hurt bad. He needs to be put down. I'm going to get my gun."

"No," Jordan cries, her face crumpling and her tears coming even faster. "You can't just shoot him. Please. Can't a vet come out and at least look at him?"

"He's in too much pain, listen to him." The deer is groaning and panting in agony, an eerie and ominous sound.

Realistically I think the man has more than one reason for wanting to get his gun. I nod at Jordan to let him go. She falls into my arms, sitting down beside me and shaking with emotion as the deer's pained cries grow louder.

I peer at the car and am astonished by the damage. The whole front end is crushed, the windshield smashed, as the vehicle hisses and creaks. After staring at it, right before my eyes, it morphs into a Humvee.

I see the carnage of a familiar scene and the bodies of my friends scattered around. Though my ears have not been damaged in this accident, here with Jordan, I suddenly can't hear. I know Jordan is talking to me again,

Danielle Stewart

I know she's screaming my name again but I can't hear her. I close my eyes to try to right myself but nothing feels real anymore. I lay my body down on the grass behind me and cover my ears as I wait for it all to disappear, and, with a flash of darkness, it does.

Chapter Eight

Jordan

I've had stitches before. In the explosion that took my sister's leg when we were children, a piece of shrapnel became lodged in my thigh. I still remember the pain as they removed it and sewed the wound. This cut on my forehead becomes an interesting metaphor for how my life has changed. As a child I was carted off to our province's makeshift hospital in the back of a truck that had previously carried goats. There had been no lidocaine, no specialist, no rubber gloves: just a man with a sewing kit and a bottle of rubbing alcohol. Even now, if I smell that, I cringe. But today, after a relatively comfortable ambulance ride, the instant delivery of pain medication, and the handiwork of a trained plastic surgeon, I'm all patched up and cared for. Well, physically anyway. Mentally I'm a wreck. I can't process what I saw out there.

It's all troubling. The shooting of an injured deer. My own blood pouring down my face. But nothing is as unnerving as what I witnessed in Click. I can't reason my way out of it. I can't make excuses. He was having a flashback. He didn't know where he was, and he could have easily killed someone if he hadn't snapped out of it in time. He could have killed me.

I haven't seen him since we were put in two different ambulances back at the accident scene. He was unconscious when they loaded him up, but I saw the man who he strangled giving an account to the police officer who arrived. I know they know what happened. What I'm not sure of, is what it means for Click.

A light knock on my door sends me jumping. I cringe at the pain radiating through my back. "Come in," I call out, convinced it's the police wanting an account of Click's behavior. I'll lie for him. I never thought I'd be that person, but for him I would.

I'm relieved and shocked to see it's Click, his nose bandaged and his eyes black and swollen.

"Are you all right?" he asks in a sad voice that breaks my heart. "They told me you got stitches, but they did a great job and you shouldn't have a scar."

"I'll be fine, how about you?" My voice is threaded with a concern that goes deeper than his physical injuries.

"Broken nose, but that's it. Some bruises from the seatbelt. A mild concussion."

He says it so casually I wonder if he forgot what happened back at the car. Does he not remember he nearly strangled a man to death? "What do you want me to tell the police?" I ask in a hushed and urgent voice.

"I already talked to them. It's going to be fine. It was an accident. They're used to this kind of thing down here by the woods. Deer are wild animals; it's bound to happen occasionally."

"That's not what I'm talking about. You attacked that man and he told the police about it. He could press charges against you."

"He's not going to. It's fine."

"How is that fine? Tell me what happened. Why did you attack him and why is it fine?" My voice is high and my words are coming frantically.

"I took a hit to the head, I was disorientated. The cop on the scene, he's a former Navy Seal. He found out my background and smoothed it over with the guy. It's not a big deal."

"Why did you attack him? What did you think was happening?"

"I don't want to talk about it, Jordan. It's over. We had a really scary thing happen today. I could have lost you. Can we please just drop it and be grateful we're both safe?"

"Are we?" I regret the words almost instantly but my adrenaline is still pumping and I can't get the image of Click's blank-eyed stare out of my mind. He was there with me lying by the car, but his mind was somewhere else.

"What do you mean?"

"Whatever you were seeing out there almost made you kill a guy. What if it were me instead of him? What if you looked at me and saw all the things you are trying to forget? Don't I look like the faces you must see in your nightmares? Aren't my features the same? Isn't my skin the same shade? What happens if you lose your bearings again and I'm the one standing in front of you?"

"Stop." Click's voice is so sharp I clutch the rails of my hospital bed, feeling uneasy. "I would never hurt you. This was an extreme circumstance. We were in a car accident. It reminded me of an accident I had when I was deployed and it set me off. I would never lay a hand on you. You have to believe that."

"I don't think for a second you would ever *knowingly* hurt me. But what happens if you wake up from one of your nightmares and don't know where you are? I wouldn't stand a chance against what I saw out there today."

Click's eyes fill with tears and it destroys me. While he manages to compose himself, I'm less successful and use my arm to wipe tears away. "What are you saying?"

He chokes out a mix of hurt and anger. "You don't want this anymore? We're done?"

"No," I shout back, sorry he thought that for even a moment. "I just think you need to get some help. I'll support you and be there for you, but I don't think you can do it on your own."

"I can't get help." He rubs his hands over his nearly shaved head as if it's about to explode.

"Why? There are resources for you. There are places you can go and people you can talk to."

"If I go and get a diagnosis or something, or they put me on pills, I can't go back."

"Go back where?"

"I can't reenlist," he says in a raspy voice as tears threaten his composure once again.

"You want to reenlist? You want to leave? You've never said that before. You never told me that. That's not fair. I deserve to know that." My breath is becoming short and panicked. A train has just run over my body.

"It's not like I have a date or something when I want to do it. I just want the option. I have brothers and sisters over there still fighting. I walked away from them. I abandoned them."

"You did your job honorably and you made a choice to move on. That's not abandonment."

"I don't expect you to understand this. That's why I've never mentioned it. I'm not reenlisting tomorrow. I know if I go to the VA and start telling them I'm seeing things, that I half-strangled a guy because I thought he blew up my Humvee, I'll never be able to go back. That option needs to be on the table for me. Even if I never take it."

"So I just have to sit back and wonder if, at any moment, you're going to make that decision? When things get tough here you might just grab your go-bag and head to the nearest recruitment office? I don't want to live that way."

"I don't know what else to tell you." Click's gaze lifts from his boots and he looks me right in the face.

"Think about it, Click. Maybe there is a damn good reason they wouldn't let you reenlist if you are having nightmares and delusions. It's for your safety and other people's safety. Looking for a loophole might not be the right solution." I'm pleading my case with reason rather than emotion.

"I had a purpose over there. I had a post that was mine to protect and missions that were mine to execute. People needed me. They needed my skills. What am I here? What am I ever going to be?"

"You could be with me. We could have a future. A life. There are jobs you could get where you could use the skills you have."

He lets out a breathy half annoyed laugh. "I don't think you know the skills I'm talking about. If you did you'd realize there aren't any civilian jobs that compare. And if there was anything remotely close, would you want to be married to a guy who risked his life to that degree every day? You'll want me working somewhere safe. You'll want what everyone wants. For me to change."

"Why did you ask me to come with you then? Why am I here if you don't see a future with me? If you have one foot out the door, why am I here?"

I watch as he thinks, and that hurts me more than any answer he can give. The fact that he has no idea why he asked me to come cuts at me. "I love you, Jordan."

"Is that enough? Because it sounds like no matter what I do, I won't fit into the life you want for yourself. So now it's my turn to ask the question. Are we done?" I'm holding back the sobs I feel rising in my chest because I don't want that changing Click's mind. I don't want sympathy to sway his decision.

"I feel better with you than without you. I'm not reenlisting tomorrow. I know it's not fair to you and I know you deserve better than I have to give right now, but please stay with me. *Please*." His demeanor shifts now from determined to desperate. His stern voice is shaking.

I've always prided myself on being the kind of woman capable of walking away from a relationship that had a downside for me. Hell, I've walked away from some just because I was too selfish to care about the other person. If I read this situation the way I'd read a business deal, I'd be gone before I hit the end of the document. But right now as I watch Click, a mess of internal conflict and need, I can't help myself. No amount of self-preservation would be enough to make me leave him right now. "I'll stay," I whisper, opening my arms to him and shifting in my hospital bed to make room. He walks over and climbs in beside me, resting his head on my shoulder as I wrap my arms around him. "I'll stay," I say again and I feel his arms come around me and squeeze tightly. Though we've settled nothing, I can't see myself walking away from him.

Chapter Nine

<u>Click</u>

"We're fine, Ma," I say into the phone for the hundredth time. "Bumps and bruises, but we'll be okay. We've already been discharged and we're back at our hotel." I have to pull the phone away from my ear as her sobs grow more dramatic. "No, you can't bring pasta fagioli to our hotel. We'll come by tomorrow for dinner. I've got to go, Ma, my other line is ringing." I hang up on my mom mid *thank the Lord my baby is alive* prayer just so I don't miss Luke's call.

"Hey Luke, got a lead for me?" I ask, and I can see Jordan leaning in to listen. She's uneasy, and rightfully so. I don't want her to worry about everything I'm doing so I pull the phone from my ear and turn on the speaker so she can hear the conversation too.

"I think I do. Your brother-in-law left his job at Safron, Inc. No activity on his credit cards or the cell phone number you gave me."

"Shit."

"But luckily I have some very creative contacts who've been able to track him down. He's staying in a motel about twenty miles from yours. He's paying cash and the room is reserved under an alias. But a car that's registered to him was issued a parking ticket a block from there about a week ago. My guy was able to make the connection. Even though he hasn't actually gotten eyes on him, he's pretty confident."

"That's great, can you text me the address?"

"Sure thing. How's everything else going?" Luke asks, likely just to be nice, not knowing the depth of that question, considering what the last twenty-four hours have been like.

"It's good," I lie, looking over at Jordan's intentionally level face. She's been stoic since we left the hospital. Luckily the rental car company dropped off another vehicle because I would have walked before I called anyone in my family for a ride. Not in the physical and emotional state we were in.

"Well keep in touch, and if you need anything else let me know. Adeline says hi, by the way. She misses you both like crazy."

"We miss her too. I really appreciate the help, Luke." As I hang up the phone, Jordan's hand slides across the bed, clutching my forearm.

"That's good news," she says, and I can't tell if it's a question or a statement. "Do you plan to go there?"

"Not tonight. Tonight I just want to order room service, watch some mindless television, and lie right here with you." I toss my phone on the nightstand, ignoring the text from Luke with the address to Jonah's hotel. I brush my finger lightly across the white bandage taped to Jordan's forehead and lean in to kiss it. "I just want to be right here tonight."

Chapter Ten

Click

The swelling in my nose has gone down, but the blotches of black and blue beneath my eyes don't look any better than they did last night. I flip up the sun visor mirror and smile over at Jordan as she does the same, inspecting her own bumps and bruises.

"Don't we make a fine pair?" she laughs, but stops suddenly when the wrinkling of her forehead causes her pain. "Ouch."

"Maybe you should have stayed back at the hotel." Seeing Jordan in pain, her body battered, reminds me how important she is. I think what today may have been like if she hadn't decided to stay with me. Would she have hopped a flight back to New York or gone back to Clover maybe? That yanks the knots in my stomach even tighter.

I want to be honest with her about how I feel, what the military means to me. But it's like we're speaking different languages. Trying to explain it to someone who has never experienced it feels impossible.

"I'm glad I came. I'm anxious to hear what your brother-in-law has to say for himself. I have to be honest, I can't think of a single explanation that would make what he's done acceptable."

"I know he must have his reasons. Jonah is a good guy. We'll find out soon. Here's the motel he's been staying in." I pull in across the street from the row of bright blue doors sunk into a long yellow structure, surrounded on all sides by alleys and run-down houses that look like they've been forgotten by the world. On our side of the street is a patch of woods with so much litter on its fringe it might as well be a trash heap. The flashing sign of the motel reads: "Vacancy—Long-term discounted rates available." I put the car in park, and when Jordan reaches for her door handle I catch her arm.

"We aren't going anywhere yet. He's supposed to be staying in room 207. It's over there." I point to the door and watch Jordan's eyes follow my finger toward it. "We're going to hang out and watch to see if he comes out. It might be hours."

"Why?" she asks, as though I'm making too big of a deal of this. What Jordan doesn't realize is even simple situations can turn into trouble if you don't prepare properly.

"Never underestimate the power of surveillance," I explain.

"Okay," she says, stretching out the word like she thinks I'm crazy. "I'm all for your plan; I just wish I had known. I would have packed a snack or something."

"There's a bag of supplies behind your seat."

Jordan reaches around and pulls my green duffle bag up onto her lap. Yanking open the zipper I see her lips curl into a confused smile. "When did you get all this stuff? Drinks, protein bars, magazines?"

"The magazines are for you. I knew you'd be bored. I went out last night while you were sleeping."

"No you didn't. I didn't hear you go out, when did you leave?"

"I specialize in coming and going without being heard. It's kind of my thing," I smirk, and she rolls her eyes at me.

"Well do you specialize in bragging so much that you miss important stuff, because someone is coming out of room 207. Is that Jonah?"

I squint my eyes and lean forward to try to get a better look. I've known him long enough to be able to spot his walk, the nuances of his gait. "That's him." I watch him hop down the iron stairs and look repeatedly over his shoulder. There's a fidgeting in his body, an uneasiness that is not part of his normal demeanor. My first thought is drugs. That would certainly explain his out-of-character behavior. These new living circumstances could all be tied to drugs.

"What's he doing?" Jordan asks as Jonah hesitates at the bottom of the stairs and stands completely frozen for a moment before turning around to go back to his room.

"I don't know. I'm going to go talk with him." I look Jordan over and realize I haven't given much thought to her safety in this. If Jonah is on drugs and acting out of his normal character then maybe confronting him isn't a good idea. But this certainly isn't an area I'd leave her alone in the car either. "Come with me but stay close and don't say anything until I have a better understanding of what's going on."

"Yes sir," she says with another roll of her eyes and a mock salute.

I grab her hand and hold it in mine, staring at her, making her understand I'm serious. "I don't know what's going on with Jonah, and this isn't a particularly safe area." I reach behind my seat and grab my weapons. I strap my knife to my ankle and clip my gun to my belt, pulling my shirt down over it.

"You really think that's going to be necessary?" Jordan asks, her eyes locked on the shiny black handle of my knife.

"I hope not." I step out of the car and round it quickly to make sure I'm at Jordan's side when she gets out. My eyes are initially on the door to Jonah's room, but something a few car lengths ahead catches my eye. A silver car with dark tinted windows and an out of state license plate is looking out of place. The car is running and the windows are partially open. I can see a man's face reflected in the side mirror as he brings a long scoped camera up to his eye for a brief second and then lowers it again.

I stop in my tracks and catch Jordan's arm so she does the same. "I need you to trust me. Do you?"

"Completely," she answers, and I'm grateful for that.

I casually slide the car keys into her hand and begin giving her instructions. "In a minute I want you to get in the car and speed off, as if we're fighting about something. Drive to that gas station we passed when we came off the main road. Do you remember it?" I wait for her to nod and try to ignore the fear growing in her eyes. "I'll meet you there in a little while. Lock the car doors and if anyone approaches you, drive off. If you're sure no one is following you then go back to our hotel."

"And if someone is following me?"

"Find a police station and beep your horn like crazy until someone comes out."

"I don't understand," she says, her voice louder than I expect it to be, considering the circumstances. I make a gesture for her to keep her voice down and twist my face to tell her she's completely blowing this. "How could you sleep with my sister?" she cries as she raises her hand and slaps my face with what feels like her full strength. My hand flies to my stinging cheek, which still hasn't completely healed from yesterday's car accident. "You can find your own damn way home you son of a bitch," she shouts as she runs to the car and does exactly what I told her to do. Though it's a slightly more dramatic performance than I expected, the screeching tires are a nice touch.

I toss my hands up in the air like a stranded person might and then start cursing. I walk past the car and take note of the license plate number, forcing myself to remember every digit. I take a seat on the bottom of the stairs that Jonah had walked down and then quickly stand up and pull out my phone. The men have taken note of me, but I seem like an annoyance rather than anything they'd be interested in.

I pretend to make a few phone calls that go unanswered and then turn my back on the men as I make the only call that matters right now. It's a quick one to the police about suspicious activity on this block. About seven minutes later the first cop car pulls up. He elicits the reaction I need to get a better read on the situation. As the blue flashing lights round the corner, the silver car slams into gear and pulls away quickly. These are not the good guys. Good guys don't run at the first sign of the police.

After a brief conversation with the officer about not seeing anything suspicious and a flash of my military identification, he's on his way. I look at the motel door that Jonah disappeared into and consider going there. But I've left Jordan alone long enough and I'm sure she's worried.

I break into a jog down the cracked sidewalk. It'll be about a mile back to that gas station, but I'm overdue for a workout anyway. My mind swirls with thoughts of Jonah and what he might have gotten himself into. And more importantly, how I'll help him get out of it.

Chapter Eleven

<u>Click</u>

"You did good," I tell Jordan as I hop in the passenger seat and lean over to kiss her cheek. She looks instantly relieved at the sight of me.

"I've spent enough time with you in Clover to see you in action. I can tell when you're serious. What happened? That silver car, they were watching Jonah too?"

"It looked like it. I called the cops and the silver car took off in a hurry when the first cruiser pulled up. That tells me they aren't likely the good guys."

"Who, well, besides us, would want to watch Jonah?"

"I got the plate and I'll have Luke see if he can track it down, though I'm sure it's a rental."

"How are we going to talk to Jonah if people are watching him?"

"*We* aren't. I can get close to him by myself without being spotted by anyone. I'll go back over there tomorrow morning but you need to stay behind."

"Excuse me, but I think my performance back there was pretty convincing. Are you saying you don't think I'll be a good partner for this?"

"Convincing might be an understatement. That slap was a little over the top. You know I have a broken nose right?"

"Listen, being undercover is a difficult job. If you aren't up for the challenge that isn't my fault."

We laugh as Jordan puts the car in gear and heads back toward the hotel. I keep tracing the profile of her face out the corner of my eye, marveling how I ended up with someone as amazing as she is. And, more importantly, I wonder how I am going to keep her.

"Do you want to take a detour?" I don't normally enjoy being spontaneous but as cool as Jordan is being, I still know I did damage to our relationship yesterday at the hospital. I know she's worried I might be teetering on the edge of reality and, at any minute, could reenlist. Both are terrifying scenarios to her.

"Sure, I'm up for another adventure, especially if I get to slap someone again. That's been my favorite part of the day so far."

I direct Jordan down the roads that lead to the one place I never thought I'd take anyone. But now, with her, maybe it's just the one place I never wanted to take anyone but her.

"Turn here." I see the unease in her eyes as the road turns from two lanes to one, and then to barely passable dirt. We haven't been by a house in nearly two miles. "Park in that clearing over there."

"Where are we, Click?" she asks as she puts the car in park and spins her head to try to get a better look around. "I'm not an outdoors kind of girl. You know that about me, right?"

"I do. This is a place I used to come when I was a kid and I've never brought anyone else here. I've never told another soul about it. I want you to see it. You might be the first person to understand." I'm nervous now that maybe she won't see this place the way I do; she'll think I'm crazy. "You should put on your sneakers."

"I didn't bring them. I just have these flats," Jordan says as she steps out of the car and looks down at her silver sparkling shoes. I pop the trunk and pull her sneakers out and hand them over with a smile.

"I grabbed them just in case."

"Boy Scout," she whispers. She laces up her sneakers and I throw my bag of supplies over my shoulder. I feel empty sometimes without the extra weight on me. There was a time, back in boot camp, when I thought I'd never survive lugging eighty pounds around. Now it's such a part of me I feel off balance without it.

Jordan loops her arm in mine as we start walking into the thick woods. I push the branches out of the way and hold them long enough for her to walk safely through. It's nearly two miles of difficult terrain before I find the spot. It's a small opening with a large stone in the middle.

"What is that?" Jordan asks, tightening her grip on my arm, and it reminds me of the first time I saw this myself. I'd almost forgotten how haunting it was.

"Have you ever heard of the Trail of Tears?" I ask as we step forward toward the rock, and I feel like I'm greeting an old friend. I crouch down and Jordan does the same, although she might be doing it just so we can stay close to each other.

"I think I learned about it in school, but I don't really remember much about it. Something with Native Americans, right?"

"Yes, in the early eighteen hundreds the government wanted to relocate all the different tribes to Indian territories and reservations. There was a route that cut right through Tennessee."

"Why did people want them moved?"

"I don't know. The same reason any of that stuff happens I guess. Ignorance and fear."

"So what are you saying? Are we standing on the Trail of Tears or something?" Jordan asks, shooting to a standing position and looking down at her feet as though something might grab her.

"Not exactly. The Trail of Tears was really just the name given to the movement itself. Not necessarily the actual path they took. Along the way, thousands of Native Americans died of exposure, disease, and starvation. They tried to call it a cultural transformation but really it was a cruel form of ethnic cleansing and segregation."

"And what does that have to do with where we are right now?" Jordan's eyes are darting from left to right, the cawing of every bird and the wind through the trees startling her.

"When I was eight years old I went camping with my friend Connor and his family. There was no way in hell my family would ever camp so I knew my only shot was if I went with my buddy. I didn't know the first thing about the woods or camping but I lied and told them I did. Connor and I started messing around and playing hide-and-seek, and before I knew it I was lost. Like, really lost. I walked until I hit this clearing and found this rock." I run my hands over the words carved into it that, at the time, meant nothing to me.

"What did you do?"

"I sat here a long time, until the sun started to go down and I got scared. It was cold, and I thought no one would ever find me. Then all of a sudden I just knew what to do. I stood up and started walking and pretty soon

I was back at the camp. I don't even remember how I got there exactly."

"That's so freaky," Jordan whispers as I watch a chill run through her body.

"I know. I thought so too. The next fall we came camping again and this time I was determined to find this place and try to understand what had happened that night—how I had found my way back. After about an hour of walking, I found it again. This time I wrote the words on this rock down in a notebook. I stood up and found my way back to camp again. When I got home I went to the library and researched everything I could.

"What does it say?" Jordan asks in a whisper as though she's afraid to disturb anything or anyone who might be present here.

"It's Cherokee, a tribe that once lived here and was forced out. It says, *To be free we walk and many die. The trail where we cried.* When I learned what had happened, what our country did to a whole population of people, I couldn't understand it. So I read. And I read and I read until every detail was seared into my mind. We camped here for three more summers and every time I came here I tried to understand. Then one day it hit me. The reason it was possible for the Native Americans to be driven out, killed, and forced to suffer is the same reason anything like that in history happened. No one was strong enough to stand up and stop it. We were camping when the towers fell. It was as if everything made sense to me then. I knew that day, the moment I was old enough I would enlist."

"That's incredible."

"I'm not superstitious or anything, but somehow I found this place every single time I came out here without really knowing where I was going. And I always found my way back to camp. I feel like this place didn't just show me where I needed to go, but it showed me who I could be. I'm good at being a Marine, Jordan. I've saved lives. I've helped people. I've stood up for those who can't stand up for themselves, and as crazy as it sounds, I feel like part of that started here."

"I understand serving your country is an enormous part of who you are. I never want to stand in the way of that. I never will." Her eyes are filled with apologies and that's not at all what I was hoping.

"I don't want to reenlist, Jordan," I admit flatly. "I don't belong back there, even if my sense of duty tries to convince me otherwise. I've given that war as much of myself as I can without losing everything completely."

"But you said—"

"I know. It's a conflict I feel inside me all the time, but I know that, likely, I'll never reenlist. It's hard though; being right here, right now, it reminds me I still want to help and protect people. I'm not willing to give that part of my life up."

"I don't think you should. Your willingness to protect everyone in Clover is the part of you I fell in love with first. It really is your calling, but maybe you have more options than you think."

"Over the years I've come out here hundreds of times to feel that connection to something and this place never disappoints. When I'm here I always get the feeling that my life has purpose and that I can make a difference. What surprised me the most about falling in love with you was you give me the exact same feeling. I never feel lost when I'm with you. This place finds a way to talk directly to my soul, and somehow so do you."

I switch from my crouching position to one knee and take her hand in mine. "Jordan, I'm sorry I don't have a ring for you, but I honestly didn't know I was going to do this until we got out here. I know my flaws are great, and I don't expect you to try to fix them for me, but I promise to work on them myself. I don't ever want to lose you. Marry me, Jordan."

"I might slap you again," Jordan says and the deadpan look on her face confuses the hell out of me. "I know we're here at your weird creepy rock and this seems like the perfect moment for this, but I don't think it is."

The breath is sucked from my lungs as her words sink in. I'd hoped for tears and tight hugs, a resounding yes.

"We're a mess, and I'm not just talking about my frizzy hair and your sweat stains from that two mile trek we took to get out here. I'm talking about us. Yesterday you were strangling a perfectly nice man because you didn't know where you were for a minute. You were fighting with your family. You're trying to solve your sister's mysterious marriage problems. Does that really seem like the right time to propose?"

"Yes." I squeeze her hand tightly. "There is absolutely no wrong time to ask you to marry me because all those things you just mentioned, they get easier when we do them together. We are better together." I pull her hand to my lips and kiss it, and as her face softens, I feel a spark of hope grow in my chest. "And don't call the rock creepy, it can hear you."

"Stop it," she begs as she slaps my shoulder and moves a few inches away from the rock. "You just caught me off guard here. I wasn't expecting this."

"There might always be something in our lives that keeps the timing from being perfect. I'm not saying we have to run off and get married right away. All I'm asking is if you can imagine spending the rest of your life with me."

Jordan drops down to her knees and presses her forehead to mine, pulling back suddenly when she remembers the bandaged cut. "Ouch." I kiss the area gently and let my lips linger there for a moment. "Click," she whispers, "I've been imagining spending the rest of my life with you since we met. I'm just worried that maybe we have too much going on."

"I have a feeling you and I are always going to have something going on. Let's not let it stop us." I stand and pull her body to mine, brushing her hair back as I kiss her lips. Her hands come up around my neck but then slide down my chest and push me away.

"We are not fooling around next to this rock," she says as she looks down at the rock as though it's alive. "I don't want to get hexed."

Chapter Twelve

Click

I'm out of the hotel room before the sun comes up, even though I know that's going to annoy Jordan when she wakes and finds I'm gone. It doesn't make sense for her to come with me today. The only way I'll be able to get close to Jonah without being seen will be if I'm alone. With my bag over my shoulder I jump into the cab and direct him back to the gas station I sent Jordan to yesterday. I'll do better to walk the mile to the motel Jonah is in. It'll give me a better chance of not being seen.

There isn't an ounce of tension in my body related to getting to Jonah. I'm not nervous about sneaking past a couple of guys doing surveillance. The only stress I'm feeling is knowing I'm going to be finding out what the hell is going on with my brother-in-law. Why would he up and leave my sister to come stay in a dive of a motel like this under an assumed name? Why would anyone be doing surveillance on him? Up to this point he's been, well, *boring*. I don't mean that in a bad way, it's just he's never been in any kind of trouble. He's steady and reliable.

Jonah is a kid who aged out of foster care and had to bust his butt to make a life for himself. He bounced around a lot but on his eighteenth birthday his real life began. It was years of working any job he could in order to get an apartment when he was old enough. He's always done the right thing, the hard things, no matter what it took.

I've cataloged everything I can think of on my jog over to the motel from the gas station. Unfortunately, I can't come up with one single explanation that would end positively for Bianca and the girls. But I know Jonah and I believe in him.

As I approach the motel I duck into the alley that exposes the windows in the back of the building. I gauge which room would be his based on the number of windows, and I start looking for a way to pull myself up. I don't plan to climb in since the windows are barred, I just need to get Jonah's attention and have him meet me somewhere, after I give him a plan to shake whoever is watching him. I pull an old recycling bin below his window and flip it over. It'll barely hold my weight but I just need something to get me high enough to pull my body onto the small ledge. With some skill and a lot of effort, I get myself up there and peer in the window, looking for a sign of Jonah.

I see through the bathroom into the rest of the motel room and there, sitting awkwardly in a chair, is Jonah. Raising my hand to tap on the glass, I stop abruptly as I hear a man's gravelly, angry voice, "That's not a good enough answer." I see the strange man step toward Jonah and punch him in the face. The force of the blow should have knocked Jonah to the ground, but as the chair nearly tips backward, it becomes obvious he's restrained in it somehow. I drop down from the ledge and hustle toward the front of the building. I don't have a plan yet, which isn't like me, but Jonah is the closest thing I've ever had to a big brother and I can't stand by and let this happen to him.

I climb quickly up the stairs and in a few adrenaline-fueled strides, I'm at his door. Rather than knock, I take a step back and kick the door in, knowing the element of surprise is my best bet. "Freeze," I shout as I pull my weapon and aim it at the man closest to Jonah. A second man in the corner shoots to his feet and makes a move for a weapon of his own before hesitating.

"You a cop?" he asks, looking from me to his partner and then back again.

"No." As the word passes my lips I use the butt of my gun to take down the first guy. When he hits his knees I put my boot on his chest and knock him hard against the wall.

The other guy charges at me and I duck, sending him flying over my shoulder and into the dresser with a thud. It's not enough to knock him out so I grab the side of his head and grip a fistful of his hair to slam him against the dresser again until his body goes limp. Pulling my knife from the holster on my ankle I cut the duct tape from Jonah's wrists and yank him to his feet. "Can you walk?" I ask, fully prepared to toss him over my shoulder if he can't. He nods his head and, with confusion in his widened eyes, follows me out the door.

We run down the metal stairs, skipping two at a time. I pull him behind a row of houses and we start weaving our way out of the neighborhood and toward a patch of woods. "Come on." I pull his arm as he starts to slow down. Those men aren't dead; they're only stunned. At some point they'll come to and be pissed. And I really don't want to have to kill anyone today. I'd prefer we get somewhere they won't likely be able to catch up with us. "Through here." We move into a clearing and then up a small cluster of rocks. "Can you climb that?" I ask, pointing to a moderately difficult next level of rocks above us.

"I can if you can," he huffs and nudges me aside to get a good footing position. I feel a small weight come off me. That is the exact answer Jonah would have given me had I asked the question before any of this had happened. It means somewhere, hopefully not buried too deep, is the guy I've always known and looked up to.

I go to his left and start climbing, matching his pace. Realistically, I could climb faster, but this isn't the two of us messing around trying to show each other up. We both need to get to the top of these rocks. That's all that matters.

When I pull myself over the last ledge I get to my feet and reach my hand down to Jonah who takes it. I lift him up and we're both breathing heavily as we brush the dust off our clothes. "Your eye is cut," I say, pointing to the spot where the man's punch had landed.

"Your nose looks broken," he shoots back, half defensive and half joking.

"It is, I got in a car accident a couple days ago. Hit a deer."

"Shit, was anyone else hurt?"

"Shut up," I snap at him. "Why the hell are we talking about my car accident? You need to tell me what the hell is going on. Why did you leave Bianca and the girls? Who were those men and what did they want from you?"

"You shouldn't have come, Click." On the inside I smile a little. Jonah is one of the few people in my family who understands why calling me by that name means something to me. He's never had a problem seeing me for who I am. "I can't tell you what's going on for the same reason I can't be with my family right now. It's dangerous. I think that scene back at the motel makes that abundantly clear."

"I don't give a shit what it is or who you think you're protecting. You need to tell me what's going on."

"No, there is no fixing this. Let's stay here until the coast is clear and then go our separate ways," Jonah suggests and I watch him run his finger over the spot his wedding ring used to be.

"What are you talking about? I'm here now. I'm going to help you."

"I'm not involving any of you. I know it's hard for you to understand how I could walk away from my life and my family but I think you know me well enough to know I didn't make that decision lightly. If there were any other way, I would do it."

"Boy, you and Bianca are perfect for each other," I grumble as I continue to scan the tree line for any sign of the men.

"What's that's supposed to mean?" Jonah asks, the sound of his wife's name has him puffed up and looking ready for a fight. It's apparent his love for her has not wavered, and that gives me some hope.

"Your wife gave me a similar speech a couple days ago about not making her choices lightly and there being no other way. But she was talking about working at a strip club for a living right now." I could clarify she's only serving drinks there but I let Jonah stew in this news, hoping it will motivate him to talk to me.

Jonah's face burns hot ember red and his teeth gnash together. "No, no way she's doing that. I left her the house to sell. I told her to move back in with your parents and let them help with the girls while she got back on her feet."

"And I suppose this is her way of telling you to go screw yourself. She didn't like your plan."

Jonah's eyes look frantic and his breath comes quickly. "You have to talk some sense into her. She can't do this. She needs to think about our daughters."

"I tried talking sense into her but she sees this as the only way she can give the girls the life they deserve. The life you promised them. She doesn't want to lose the house and she sure as hell doesn't want to move in with our parents. So since she didn't listen to me, I thought maybe you would. That's why I tracked you down, so I can help you get your family back."

"I'm sorry, Click, but I'm not bringing you in on this. It's too big and I've worked really hard to distance myself from all of you so the girls stay safe. The only thing you can do is," he draws in a deep breath and turns his eyes up toward the clouds, "take care of my girls for me."

"You really think you're going to make it on your own out there? You weren't doing too well without me. Or did you forget about being duct-taped to a chair? You couldn't outrun them the first time, and they'll come after you twice as hard now.

Jonah's head drops low now and he kicks at a pebble under his feet. "I wasn't trying to outrun them, Click. If I'm running then they are looking for ways to exploit my weaknesses. They are looking for the people who I'd do anything to protect. If I'm running then Bianca is in more danger."

"Wait, so you're saying instead you're sacrificing yourself? You aren't even trying to evade them?"

"I'm not. But I had a plan."

"Cut the bullshit, Jonah." I'm nose to nose with him and I can tell by the fire in his eyes there is nothing I'll be able to say to change his mind. He's unwavering in his plan.

"When you were deployed there were plenty of times you couldn't tell us where you were. You did that to keep all your men safe. I don't dare compare what I'm doing to anything you've done. I'm not admirable in any way. But I am trying to do this for the right reason, which is to protect my family. If I'm easy to find they won't need to leverage anyone I love to get to me. You are a link back to your sister and my daughters. I can't take that risk."

"I can't let you just turn yourself over to these guys. Maybe if you tell me what's going on, I can try to find a way to help." My voice is pleading now. For a moment I'm not the war-hardened Marine, I'm the kid who looked up to Jonah for more than half my life. I respect his desire to protect his family, *my family*, but there has to be another option. I don't want to quit on him.

"Just take care of them. I know it's a lot to ask. Bianca is a handful," Jonah's words catch in his throat as he tries to dam up his emotions.

"I'm sorry." My head is low, my eyes turned down. "I'm sorry, but it's not going to happen. You might not want to tell me what's going on and you might not want my help, but you don't have a choice. Bianca is my sister and bailed on her. She deserves answers. She deserves a hell of a lot more than that. You know nothing about the life I've been living for the last six years. You don't know what I'm capable of."

"You don't know what these people chasing me are capable of," Jonah snaps through grinding teeth. "I'm in deep. Too deep."

"You don't know too deep. Too deep is when bullets are flying by your head while you're hunkered down trying to hold your position until air support can arrive. Too deep is taking down a target you've been hunting for two months and realizing suddenly you don't have a clear exit strategy." I pull in a long breath, knowing what I might be willing to admit here could change Jonah's mind, even if I don't feel ready to say it. "Too deep is feeling your Humvee explode around you and knowing it's impossible for all of your men to have survived it."

"Click," Jonah shakes his head and I can see the conflict raging inside of him.

"I've made it through harder fights than this. I can help you. You just need to tell me what's going on." The snapping of a branch in the distance draws my attention and I drop to a squatting position, signaling for Jonah to do the same. I pull my weapon and strain to interpret any other sounds. The chatter of two men rises up from the quiet woods and then trails off, getting farther away. When I'm confident they've headed in the other direction I holster my weapon and sit down on the rocks. We have a good line of sight from up here; I've always been partial to taking a position on higher ground.

"We stay here until we're sure they've moved on and then we head out. I'll have a car here to pick us up once we know it's clear. You don't have to tell me everything right now, Jonah, but I'm not letting you do this on your own."

Jonah takes a seat next to me and rubs at his wrists where the duct tape had held him to the chair. "Fine, I'll go with you today, but that's all I'll agree to right now."

"Good, I really didn't want to have to knock you out and carry you off these rocks." I throw my shoulder hard into his and he shoves me back.

"Thanks," he grunts as he settles back on the rocks and stares up to the sky.

"We'll figure this out," I try to assure him, but really I'm talking more to myself.

Chapter Thirteen

<u>Click</u>

Moving stealthily down the rocks and through the small patch of woods reminds me of being deployed. The terrain and the enemy are completely different, but the adrenaline coursing through me is identical. There's been no movement in the woods for two hours and we're heading in the opposite direction of where the two men went.

My plan is to make it back to the residential area and direct Jordan, who I've called and prepped, to a quiet backstreet to pick us up. I'm actually worried about how excited she sounded to be our get-away driver. There wasn't an ounce of hesitation or even fear in her voice.

We make our way to the edge of the woods and stop, both completely silent and waiting for any kind of unwelcomed noise. The rumbling of a distant truck engine is all I can hear. I signal that on the count of three we'll make a break for it across the street and into the neighborhood. Jonah pulls in a deep breath and puts a steely, determined look on his face as I count it out on my hand and we move. He's fast, nearly as fast as I am, and we're down behind a shed in a matter of seconds.

Pulling out my cell phone, I call Jordan and give her the information to find us. Again, she's calm as can be as I rattle off the instructions and, before I know it, she's driving up. Jonah and I rush toward the car and hop in. Our doors aren't even shut before Jordan is punching the gas and we're speeding down the street.

"You did good," I tell her from the passenger seat, patting her leg and smiling wide.

"I wish you'd stop looking so damn surprised when you say that. I can handle myself. It shouldn't come as a shock."

I lean across the center console and kiss her cheek, more in love with her now than ever before.

"So what's going on?" she asks, playfully shooing me off. "Are you both okay?"

"We're fine. When I got to Jonah's motel two guys had tied him to a chair, and he was getting his ass beaten. I broke in, knocked the guys out, and cut him loose so we could get away."

"Don't make yourself sound so badass in that story and me sound like such a chump," Jonah cuts in as he leans forward and shoves me.

"Wait, so who are the guys?" Jordan asks, furrowing her brows nervously at both of us.

"No clue, the chump won't tell me who they are or what they want from him. He's just decided to sacrifice himself to them rather than let me help."

"What?" Jordan shoots back as she narrows her eyes at Jonah in the rearview mirror for a moment. "So you still don't know what's going on? You saved his ass and he can't even tell you why it was necessary?"

"Why are you talking about me like I'm not here?" Jonah grumbles as he sticks his head up in the front seat between us.

"Unless you want to tell me what's going on, I'm going to treat you as though you don't exist, because you aren't offering me anything."

"We're two smart people, Click, I'm sure we can figure this out on our own if we try. What do we know so far?" Jordan asks, and I can see her raise an eyebrow as she glances back to Jonah, searching for his reaction.

"Your brother-in-law who, by all accounts, has otherwise lived an uneventful life has abruptly begun acting out of character. He abandoned his wife and children and cleared out the family bank account, leaving them with no safety net. He moves into a motel only thirty miles outside of town under an alias. Though he's aware he's being watched, he doesn't make an effort to leave or evade the people interested in him. So he's either a cold and heartless man who is also too stupid to know how to keep from being caught, or there is something more going on here."

"She's fun," Jonah mutters as he crosses his arms over his chest and falls hard against the back seat in frustration. "Where'd you pick her up? Did she flunk out of detective school or something?"

"You're right, Jordan," I say, continuing to ignore Jonah, mostly for the effect I know it will have on him. "The guys chasing him looked like hired thugs. I'm guessing he either got in over his head gambling or it's drugs."

"Good theories," Jordan says, nodding in agreement. "Drugs and gambling debt can be motives for erratic behavior and sudden personality changes. I learned that in detective school. He seems to be fairly lucid, however. Did you see any physical signs of drug use?"

"No, unless he's shooting up between his toes, which is a possibility. I didn't notice any track marks on his arms. Though he seems paranoid, I think it has more to do with the situation than any substance abuse."

"Let's cross that off the list then. I'm leaning more toward gambling debt. That could account for the draining of his family's bank account, the men chasing him, and the poor choices."

"I'm not making poor choices," Jonah snaps. "I'm not on drugs and don't have any gambling debt."

"Have you known him to have a history of gambling?" Jordan asks, completely ignoring Jonah's statements.

"We used to bet on college football games back in the day. He was pretty competitive about it." I point my finger up in the air as though that memory is a *eureka* moment.

"Click, I'm not in gambling debt. I'm not some lowlife who traded my family for an addiction. I'm trying to help people, other families." Jonah's voice is angry now and his defensive tone is growing.

"When confronted, if he was to be completely indignant of such suggestions, what would that tell us?" Jordan asks me, and, while none of this is a laughing matter, the combination of her seriousness and Jonah's red-faced anger is pushing me toward the edge of smiling.

"I don't know," I shrug.

"Tell me more about him, where does he work again?"

"He works for a tobacco distributor."

"What does he do there?"

"I have no clue." I turn to look at Jonah and consider asking him, but I'm met with is his middle finger in the air. "I think maybe he's in sales there? I know it's one of the oldest distributers in the state."

"The tobacco industry has been hit pretty hard over the last decade. There has been an enormous amount of litigation, higher taxes, stronger restrictions on marketing techniques, and better health education that has fewer kids starting to smoke. Combine that with more accessibility to medication and alternatives that get people to quit and that makes for the kind of business that could be struggling to turn a profit."

"I don't know, exporting tobacco is still really lucrative in Tennessee. It employs a lot of people," I add, not sure where she is going with this.

"Probably for most companies who have changed with the times, but it's normally the dinosaurs, the original companies, that struggle most with change. If they don't evolve, they falter. Do you know what struggling companies do?"

Out of the corner of my eye I can see the blood from Jonah's face draining. This is striking a chord. "What?" I ask Jordan.

"They react like cornered animals. They make bad choices and unethical decisions just to try to stay in the game. They break laws and they cut corners. At my old job we handled this all the time. Companies would bury themselves in wrongdoing and then be forced to sell to a company like mine who could make their past disappear. I've seen some appalling practices out of some desperate organizations. And do you know what those companies always have?"

"What?" I ask again, now turning to look at Jonah head on. I want to read his reaction when Jordan gives me the answer.

"They always have a whistle blower. That's normally why they come to us. Nothing is more dangerous to a company than an employee with a conscience. Someone trying to *help other families*. For example, the kind of person who would be insulted by the accusation of drug use and gambling. The kind of person who would walk away from his family just to ensure they are protected. That's the kind of a person a company is afraid of. Especially if they have concrete evidence of wrongdoing. They wouldn't hesitate to send some thugs out to try to deter the person from exposing the information they have. Some companies will stop at nothing to quiet them."

The car falls completely silent as Jordan pulls into the parking lot of our hotel.

"I guess I was wrong about detective school. You wouldn't have flunked out," Jonah says with a deadpan look on his face as he rests his exhausted head on the cool car window.

Chapter Fourteen

<u>Jordan</u>

I tip the man at the hotel for bringing up a cot and tell Click for the hundredth time that I don't mind sharing our room with Jonah. It's no big deal. We won't be screwing like wild animals on the desk tonight, but I think we can survive. The time we spent in Clover has taken away most of my anxiety about being with people. I can deal with a few nights in a cramped hotel room especially if it means getting to the bottom of Jonah's problem. Now that I think it has something to do with his company, I'm thoroughly intrigued.

I watch as Jonah spins the top off another small bottle from the mini bar and wonder how drunk he plans to get. "Do you need a few more of those before you're going to tell us what you know about your company?" I ask, raising my brows with attitude.

"I'm not telling anyone anything. I have a plan." There is a slur in Jonah's now cocky voice and I can see that last mini bottle of booze likely made him useless for the rest of the night. "I didn't drain our bank account so Bianca and the kids had nothing. I hate myself for doing it. But I needed them to look wronged by me. I needed them to have little to nothing of worth so these assholes didn't think they were profiting from anything I was doing. The fools still think this is about money. They believe I'm after some blackmail payout. They are under the impression I did what I did and bailed on my family so I can profit. That's what I need them to think so they'll leave Bianca and the girls alone."

"And turning yourself over to them? Giving up?"

"I have a failsafe in place: if anything happens to me the information is released to the proper channels. I wanted them to hear that from me. I needed to get caught to be able to tell them. I needed them to see I had no contact with Bianca and there would be no point in going after her to get to me."

"And if they'd have killed you?" Click asks angrily.

"Then the information would have been released, Bianca and the girls wouldn't have been targeted, and I'd die knowing that."

"Well they didn't kill you so you were going to . . . what? Run? Never look back?" Click's accusatory tone is grating on Jonah's drunk and fragile patience.

"No, I was buying some time, trying to get in touch with people who could protect us in exchange for the information I have. I had planned to make those contacts first but I got found out. I had to distance myself from everyone and look as though I didn't care about them. It's the hardest thing I've ever had to do."

"Have you made any contacts yet?" I ask, my business antennas going up. This is very much a part of the corporate world I'd worked in for years. I know people like Jonah, and I've been on both sides of what he is trying to do.

"No, the lobbyists and bureaucrats my company employs are far reaching. I can't tell who is in their pocket and who is legit. Everyone I thought I could trust, people I worked with for years, betrayed me. I'm still trying to figure out who I can go to without creating more risk."

"Your plan is shit," I say as I grab the bottle from his hand, pour the rest of it into the small glass tumbler, and quickly drink it down. He looks shocked by my blunt language. "You have no contacts, no real protection, and no way of getting out of this. If these guys are serious, they won't care if you will or won't cave when your family is in jeopardy. They figure it will be worth a try. You're in over your head."

"How exactly do you know anything about this?" Jonah shouts angrily.

"Because, while I may not have been the person strapping the guy to a chair and trying to get information out of him, I've had my share of isolating and defusing situations like this. I've dealt with the whistle blowers, and I know how seriously a company takes a threat like you. The greater the cost is to the company, the greater the risk to you. Maybe the tactics are different down here, but I'm guessing since they're willing to cause bodily harm this means you've got something crippling on them."

"You have a better plan?" Click asks hopefully as he tries breaking the mounting tension between Jonah and me.

"I do. I have contacts in New York who will jump on this if your information is credible. There are agencies who deal specifically with different types of ethical and environmental infringements. If you tell me what information you have I'll find the right person to help you."

"And my family?"

"They'll likely need to be protected while the process moves forward. Maybe even long term." I avert my eyes while explaining this. No one wants to think about living that way for an extended period of time, but it's reality.

"No, I'm not going to do that to them. I'm not going to have them move or change their names because of something I've started."

"Unfortunately the need for that already exists. Every minute you don't make these decisions, the more dangerous this becomes. The longer you hold this information, the more desperate the company will get." I hate to be the one to break this news but someone has to.

"And where do I draw the line? Who in my family is safe and who isn't? Bianca's sisters and their kids—are they safe? Her parents?"

"I don't know," I admit. "I don't know to what length your company will go to resolve this and keep the information from being leaked. I don't know enough right now. You need to tell me. Are we talking about lawsuits they'll pay their way out of? Are we talking about environmental penalties that will crush their bottom line and put them out of business?"

"I'm not telling you. I don't even know you."

"You know me," Click says, stepping forward with a frustrated tone. "You've known me forever and you know you can trust me. We've always trusted each other."

"So by proxy I'm just supposed to trust your girlfriend?"

"No, but you can trust my fiancée, the woman I'm going to marry. You can trust her, because I do." Click and I haven't really discussed our relationship status since we left the woods yesterday. I didn't shout *yes* from a mountaintop but I didn't say no either. It's the first time I hear him call me his fiancée and it catches me off guard.

"And how long have you even known her? You haven't even been home that long. You run off to do some job somewhere in North Carolina and she comes back with you. That's not enough for me. You could be blinded by a sexy figure and a great smile."

In one impressive movement, Click kicks the chair Jonah is sitting in backward so it slams against the desk and tilts back on two legs. "I'm not blinded by anything. I trust Jordan with my life. You're acting like an idiot right now and my patience is getting thin. So cut the shit and tell us what information you have."

Jonah slams the chair back down on all four legs and jumps to his feet, nose to nose with Click. "I didn't ask you for help. You just have to play hero like usual. You never need anyone. You're always bailing everyone out."

"I've needed you a thousand times, and you've always come through," Click says, shoving him backward and back down into the chair.

Jonah doesn't make a move to stand again. I'm grateful for that because, while I consider myself a very capable woman, breaking up a fistfight between these two wouldn't be easy.

"You walk around like you can solve everything, like you don't ever need help. It's aggravating as shit," Jonah mumbles as he hangs his tired head.

"Two days ago I crashed my car, that's why we look like this," Clicks says, pointing to his face and then the cut on my head. "It was an accident. A deer ran out from the woods. But you know what? When it was over I didn't know where I was. I thought I was still deployed. I thought I was back there on the day my Humvee hit an IED, and half my guys were blown up. I thought the enemy was closing in on us and I nearly strangled a man to death. Some poor guy who heard the accident and crossed his property to come make sure we were all right.

If Jordan hadn't snapped me out of it I might have killed him. Every night I go back there. Every night it haunts me. I need help, but you're right, I haven't had the balls to ask for it yet."

"I didn't know," Jonah sighs in a mix of anger and empathy. "I didn't realize you were going through that."

"I left behind a lot of people there. Some will never come home in one piece. I could use the one guy I've always thought of as a brother to have my back right now. Let us help you get through this so you can be around when I need you."

Jonah spins the top off another small bottle of alcohol and takes it all into his mouth in one swig. He swallows it down with a pained look on his face.

"I want to keep Bianca and the girls safe," he says, tipping his head back and staring up at the ceiling.

"Then Jordan and I are your best chance."

Chapter Fifteen

<u>Jordan</u>

"I need to know everything to connect you with the right people. Are we talking environmental, ethical, or personnel infractions?" I ask, sitting on the edge of the bed next to Click and waiting for Jonah to answer.

"All of the above," a now somewhat sober Jonah says as he takes a swig of hot coffee. Once Click and I convinced him to stop drinking and eat some decent food, the conversation became more productive. "And it's not just limited to Safron, Inc. There are six major distributors of tobacco in the south. I've been able to find incriminating evidence on four of them. I'd imagine the other two are involved but have done a better job of covering their tracks."

"So give me some examples and tell me how you came across the evidence," I say as I pull out a notebook and start jotting things down.

"I've worked for them since I was eighteen years old. The company was well established even back then but they still had a good ol' boys atmosphere and some of the head guys took me under their wings. I moved up the ladder pretty quickly for a kid who didn't go to college. Last year I was promoted to Director of Public Relations. I was reluctant, considering I was in sales my entire career, and didn't particularly want to be the face of the company or deal with any of those issues. But the money they offered was persuasive. We were doing alright financially with Bianca giving dance lessons part time, but we weren't putting away as much money as we should have been. I just wanted my kids to have a chance to have more than I had. I wanted Bianca to have the job she loved, even though it didn't bring in much money, without having to feel bad."

He drops his heavy head into his hand and groans in frustration. I know he's thinking, as I am, how far from that Bianca is right now. "It wasn't long before I realized the job was an empty token position; I literally didn't do anything for the first month. When I approached the vice president of the company he told me I'd be plenty busy in the near future and to just keep showing up for work. Then one day I was so bored I started digging around and found dozens of documents with my signature on them. Things I'd never signed. Things I'd never even seen."

"They were setting you up to be the scapegoat?" I ask, feeling a small pang of guilt for having done this to people in my own cutthroat past. Not to the extent of forging anyone's name but just setting up the pins and letting the scapegoats knock them down. People walked right into the traps that were set for them.

"Exactly. Those documents were associated with a clinical study regarding the effectiveness of a drug used to help patients stop smoking. They were instructing lobbyists to interfere with the studies and skew the results. Planting fake patients and doctors on our payroll. When I dug deep enough I found there were memos from outside parties who had grown suspicious. They were coming in right around the time I'd been appointed to my new job, though on paper the company had backdated my promotion to make me culpable for these documents. They were setting me up."

"Why would they choose you for something like this? You've been a part of the company for so long,"

Click says, clearly wracking his brain to make sense of this.

"I've always been a little bit on the outside there. I've got no higher education and no pedigreed upbringing. I think they've always thought of me as a hard worker and an asset but never as one of them," Jonah explains, trying not to appear bothered.

"Interfering with a clinical trial is serious business, but it's not a large enough scale to really impact a company the size of Safron, Inc., is it?" Click asks, directing his question at me rather than Jonah.

"It shouldn't be enough, though it might warrant further investigation, which could result in more infractions found." I try to put a positive spin on the complicated situation.

"That's not even the evidence I have," Jonah says, perking back up as though he finally feels eager to share. "It's so much deeper than that. Once I knew I was being set up it changed everything for me. I didn't confront anyone. I dug deeper. I found so many secrets. They've interfered, either through lobbyists or directly, with hundreds of clinical studies, ranging from drugs used to help quit smoking to inflating the side effects associated with vapor cigarettes. You know, the ones that don't use tobacco. They spread those results like propaganda through every outlet they could. In the last six months it impacted the sales of those products by over twenty percent."

I bite at my lip as I realize who will be the best contact for dealing with this information. I'd been so good at separating my work life from my personal life over the years, but Wes Grimley was one of the few exceptions. We worked together when my company acquired a medical research and development company that had lied in order to sell a product so they could stay in the black. They were on the verge of being exposed when my company swept in with the promise of running damage control then turning a profit. Wes was my contact at the FDA and we worked closely for weeks trying to sort out how to separate the very valuable clean data from the false and misleading data. I, of course, was trying to invest the least amount of my company's money while Wes was trying to scrutinize every detail. That's his job. It was heavy negotiations and lots of arguing. We were both cut from the same cloth in many ways, though we were fighting for different sides. Ultimately when he asked me out, against my better judgment I said yes. I think I'd confused the chemistry we had at work for something it wasn't. A knot is tightening in my stomach as I realize he's likely the best person to contact to help Jonah with this part of the scandal. He's incredible at his job and well respected in his field.

"Well I have one contact at the FDA Compliance and Regulatory Office. With enough evidence he could blow up the scandal. It could be enough to take down the hierarchy at the company, maybe rattle investors. But it's not likely to catch everyone involved in that net," I offer, putting aside my own messy history with Wes and trying to look at the bigger picture.

"There is more, so much more," Jonah says, taking in another swig of his coffee. "There is environmental stuff too. With the impact to the bottom line from the changes in the industry, every one of our plants has begun to cut corners. Small at first but now it's out of control. They're dumping waste products, and there is extreme runoff from at least two of the plants that have destroyed a large area and contaminated drinking water for two counties. They're paying off the officials in charge to keep it quiet. No one has caught on to the statistics yet, but it's impacting the health of many of the people who live in those areas."

"That's big," I agree. Jonah's energy is feeding my resolve to help him with this. "I've worked very closely with the EPA over the years. We've invested in a lot of companies with significant issues that needed to be cleaned up. Nothing as bad as you're saying, but I have people who'd be very interested in breaking this case open, too."

"How do you know you can trust these people? What if they can be bought?"

"Trust me, they can't be."

"But how do you know?" Jonah stresses.

"Because I was on the team that, in one way or another, tried to buy them. These people never played ball. No matter how much my company tried to strike deals they always stuck to their ethics. They're straight shooters and dedicated to their job." I consider casually stating that I'd dated someone who could assist. Guilt is threatening to swallow me up, as I omit this information.

"Wait, so you used to be like the people at Safron? Trying to play the system and hurt people?" Jonah asks, and I can feel Click leaning in, ready to come to my defense. I cut in before it becomes necessary.

"I was responsible for making my company money and protecting them from scandals. I never sent any thugs after anyone, I never paid someone to overlook dangerous drinking water, but I walked that fine line. When I met Click in Clover I saw a glimpse of a small town that could either be crushed or saved. That power was in my hands and it changed me. I'm not proud of my career up until then, but I made the right choice. And the one benefit I have is, along the way, though they were thorns in my side at the time, I met a lot of influential people who were trying to do the right thing. I know they'd be ecstatic to hear from me with this kind of information for a change."

That might be a bit of a stretch as far as Wes is concerned. After a couple months of dating I stopped returning his calls. I completely blew him off. I'd been assigned to my next project and the sparks between us were truly just limited to the work we were doing together. When the back and forth tug between us no longer had a purpose, things fizzled out. I could have handled it better, but it wasn't in my nature to deal with other people's feelings very well. I'm hoping now that I've evolved he'll be able to see that and whatever old tension might be between us will take a back seat to this incredible industry-changing information I'll bring him.

"There is one more thing. The tobacco industry changed dramatically in the nineties when litigation took place and required cigarette packages to carry labels warning of health and addiction risks. Prior to that, these companies had more money than they knew what to do with. When the crackdowns began, Safron fell in line with the rest, or at least they appeared to. They changed their marketing campaigns in order to look as though they weren't still targeting kids. They paid out every lawsuit and adhered to every tax increase and legal stipulation. But over the last few years, they've been pulling the strings and getting officials put in strategic positions in order to regain some of the foothold they've lost. They're desperate."

"What other types of things have they done? Do you have more evidence?" I ask, scratching things down in my notebook again.

"They've begun shifting the formula in their products. Slowly increasing the amount of nicotine and, in turn, making them more addictive. They've found a way to get all of this past the FDA."

"That's a good way to keep yourself in business. Get more people hooked," Click says with a grimace.

"Exactly. It's all regulated, but over time they've handpicked and paid off the regulators. It's been a slow process, and, judging by the information I found, it was painstaking, but it has paid off. They've made back the billions they were losing. I have a flash drive with documented internal memos, lists of lobbyists and officials on the payroll. I spent three months gathering every ounce of proof I could while acting like the dope they needed me to be."

"You did a fantastic job," I tell Jonah. I miss some of the excitement associated with the work I used to do. While I haven't spent much time on the admirable side of things, I know I'm good at what I do, and I feel like I could really help.

"Now the real work begins," Click says clapping his hands together. "Someone needs to convince Bianca and the rest of my family for their own protection they need to leave Sturbridge."

"Where will they go?"

"Hopefully when the ball gets rolling the federal agencies involved will help provide protection, but in the meantime I have a beach house in Florida they could stay in. No one knows I own the property. I keep it as a little spot I can run away to if needed." I feel Click's eyes dart toward me as I explain this.

"I didn't know that you had that," Click says, looking a little hurt as though I've kept it a secret on purpose. His reaction confirms that telling him about my history with Wes is a bad idea.

"It'll be big enough for everyone?" Jonah asks; saving me from having to give Click any kind of explanation for why I hadn't mentioned the property.

"It'll be tight, but we're only talking a few days to a week, I hope."

"Ma will never go for this. She'd rather set her house up like a fort and defend it to the death than leave all her precious stuff there," Click offers, and I get a lump in my throat thinking about how much Corinne will hate everything I have at the beach house. It will surely not be good enough.

"I can convince your mom if you take a crack at Bianca. She won't have anything to say to me right now," Jonah says, looking sad at the thought of his wife and the status of their current relationship.

"Looks like you two have your work cut out," I laugh and begin planning where I can be when Corinne is told of this plan, because I sure as hell don't want to be at her house.

"I'm not sure what you think is so funny. You're coming with us to tell them," Click asserts and Jonah nods his head in agreement.

"Great," I grumble as I roll my eyes. "They already hate me."

"They don't hate you," Jonah interjects with some warm empathy in his eyes.

"How do you know? You haven't been at the disastrous dinners."

"Trust me, if they hated you, they'd have run you out of Tennessee by now. The fact that you're still welcomed back at their house is telling. I got kicked out weekly when Bianca and I first started dating."

"How comforting."

"Now, after you tell them they have to pack their bags and leave town, they might hate you." Click laughs as he exchanges a funny look with Jonah.

"If it counts for anything, I hate both of you." I throw a punch into Click's shoulder and immediately regret it. It certainly hurt my hand more than it did the rock-hard muscle of his arm. I fall back onto the bed and hold my aching hand and pout. "Jerks!"

Chapter Sixteen

Click

As I tap lightly on the door of my sister's rundown apartment I feel like throwing up. I can't imagine what she'll do when she opens the door to find Jordan and me with Jonah in tow. Our only chance at her being remotely less than homicidal is if the girls are there. Bianca has her flaws, but the one thing she's always taken very seriously is her job as a mother. I think when you're raised by parents like ours, there are a lot of benefits, but you also learn what not to do. Bianca has always made a point not to argue too much in front of her girls. My parents didn't abide by that code and it drove all of us nuts at times. I can only hope she can hold true to that now.

The hinges creak as Bianca pulls open the door. As I quickly open my mouth to explain, trying to beat her to the rage that burns in her eyes, something I didn't plan happens. Daphne squeezes by her mother's legs and shoves past me. She dives into her father's arms and squeals with joy.

"Baby," Jonah gasps as he crouches down and clutches desperately at his daughter. In a flash, Penny is charging toward him, and I watch his eyes glass over with tears. They look so very much like Jonah that when the three of them are squeezed together you feel like you're looking at a puzzle with the pieces placed in the right spot.

Bianca grabs the collar of my shirt and yanks me inside with the full force of her strength. "What the hell is going on here? How could you bring him here? How could you let the girls see him?" The hiss in her hushed voice is cutting at me, and she's looking as though I've just betrayed her.

"Give him a chance to explain," I plead, but she peers around to make sure her children are still distracted by the joy of seeing their father, and then she slaps me hard across the face.

"Bastard," she mutters, wiping a tear from her cheek.

Jordan steps into the apartment but doesn't say a word. Even she knows better than to try to plead our case while Bianca is reeling.

"B, please let me talk to you for a minute," Jonah begs, both his girls scooped up in his arms and snuggling his neck.

"Not in front of the girls," is all she can muster before she bites down hard on her lip and fights every urge to lash out. "Girls, I know you're excited that Daddy is here but I need to talk to him for a minute. Go to your room, please." The girls whine in protest and clutch harder to their dad's neck as Bianca begins counting to three in the threatening tone only a mother can deliver.

Jonah wiggles them down his body in a silly manner and puts them back on their feet. "Listen to your mother. Go to your room and gather up your things because we're leaving. We're going on vacation." When the girls skitter away and round the corner to their bedrooms, Jonah steps inside and is met with the furious fists of Bianca flying toward him. I grab her by the waist and take multiple blows to the head and chest as I try to calm her.

"He was trying to protect you," I call as I bring her hands down to her sides and hold them there. She leverages my position to lift her body and starts kicking in Jonah's direction instead.

"I don't care what he was doing or what he told you; there is *nothing* on this earth that justifies what he did to us. Now you get him out of here while I think of a way to keep my daughters' hearts from breaking all over again."

"We have to leave," Jordan says quietly, like she's trying to calm an unruly animal. "I know you're upset, and rightfully so, but if you want to keep your daughters safe then please listen."

Bianca's body relaxes slightly at the thought of her daughters possibly being in danger. But she still looks ready to strike if needed.

"Pack up, Bianca, everything you and the girls will need for a few weeks. I'll explain on the way," I demand as I start to gather up some things from the coffee table next to me.

"You've lost the right to give me advice or tell me what to do. Bringing him here like this, you betrayed me. The only reason I'm even listening to any of you right now is because you're playing the one card I can't ignore. You know I will do anything to protect my children. It's a damn good thing too, because apparently I'm the only parent willing to."

"Bianca, there are people who will hurt us, all of us, if we don't get out of here now," Jonah begs as he reaches a hand out toward her face, but she slaps it away. "Let me explain."

"There is nothing, not one single thing you could explain to me right now that would change anything. If you're saying you abandoned us for our own good, our protection, fine. What a hero you are. It changes nothing for me because if the situation were reversed, I'd have found another way. Or at the least, I would have given you some kind of explanation. But you can save it now;

it's too late." Bianca turns on her heels and heads away from us. The sound of her opening and shutting her dresser drawer is the only indication that she's actually doing what we've asked her.

"I'll go help the girls pack up," Jordan offers as she slinks away from us, also feeling like crap about this whole thing.

When everything is loaded in the two cars, I wait to see how we'll split the group.

"Bianca, will you ride with me so I can explain?" Jonah asks with a desperate voice.

"We'll take the girls in our car. Jordan and I would be happy to take them so you and Jonah can ride together," I offer, but she shoots me a deathly look and I step back quickly as though she could kill me with her eyes.

"No. Jordan and I can take the girls. Uncle Click and Daddy should ride together," Bianca asserts, looking as though nothing will change her mind.

"I want to go with Daddy," Daphne pouts as she clutches Jonah's leg possessively. "I don't want to go with you and Jordan."

"How about you ride with me and your mom," I say, scooping her up into my arms and tickling her. "You love hanging with Uncle. We're all going to Nona's anyway. Jordan and your daddy will ride together, and we'll all be there in no time."

"Whatever," Bianca huffs and we split up. Jordan and Jonah climb in our rental car and Bianca, the girls, and I get in the family car. I don't feel bad about sending Jordan and Jonah off in the car alone together. They'll have plenty to talk about relating to the business matters. Plus, if Bianca doesn't want to hear it from her husband, I want time alone with my sister to try to get through to her.

"Put your headphones on girls and Mommy will put in a movie," Bianca instructs as she flips down the small DVD player and the girls strap themselves in.

When we back out of the driveway, and I'm certain the girls are engrossed in their movie, I make an attempt at smoothing things over.

"He found information that his company was breaking the law and putting people's health in danger. He wanted to expose them but keep you safe so he distanced himself and made it look as though he'd abandoned you." I blurt the words out before she can protest, and she's furious at the way I've delivered the news.

"Shut up," she barks, slamming her hand down on the steering wheel. "I don't want to know. I was his partner and his best friend. Whatever it was he should have trusted me with the truth right from the beginning. Now I'm doing what you've asked of me, reluctantly, but I am. If there is danger, then for the sake of my kids I'll listen to you. But you don't get to tell me how to feel about my husband."

I reach into my pocket and feel the edge of an envelope that's been as much a part of me over the last six years as my weapon. It's seen as much combat as I have and it's as weathered as I am. Pulling it out, it grabs Bianca's attention but then she hardens her face, looking uninterested.

"Do you know what this is?" I ask, bringing the letter up for her to see it. I tear open the envelope and, though I'm flooded with emotion, I push myself to continue. I'm not comfortable sharing this. It takes me back to somewhere I never wanted to be mentally, but I feel like it might help Bianca forgive Jonah.

"What?" she asks with a huff and glances at the folded paper.

"It's my *if you're reading this* letter. Most deployed people have them. It's a message for the people we love in case anything should happen to us. I've carried around and mailed more than I'd like to admit for friends I've lost. I even hand delivered one, which makes the list of the hardest things I've ever had to do. And here is mine."

"Why are you showing me that? It's morbid. You're home now, you don't need that anymore," Bianca snaps.

"I'm showing it to you because it's important for you to know who I addressed it to. You'd think Ma, right? But it's not. I didn't think there would be anything I could say in one letter to bring her peace if anything happened to me."

"So who then?"

"It's addressed to Jonah." I flip the envelope over and show her the tattered paper with his name across the front. "I wrote it after being in Fallujah for two weeks. I thought the whole idea of having these letters was a bad omen. But after seeing how things were over there, I sat my ass down and started writing."

"Why would you send it to him and not one of us? Or Dad?"

I unfold the papers and beat back the voices in my head begging me not to read this. These words were written by a naïve kid. A scared, newly deployed kid I don't know anymore. As much as I've tried to bury my feelings, this will certainly uproot some. It's worth it for Bianca though. I clear my throat as I start to read.

"Dear Jonah,

I feel bad for putting this burden on you but I know you're tough enough. I don't know anyone stronger than you. You've survived my family so I know you can handle this.

"I didn't think I'd write one of these letters but with everything going on here, I realize, I'd better. Somewhere in my mind I've always known that tomorrow isn't promised to us, but being out here, that idea is an ever-present and lurking reality. I thought for a long time about who to send this to, but it's clear you're the only person I know who can handle this responsibility. Just like you've handled everything you've ever had to do.

"When I really sit down and reflect on my life up to this point I see how much of an unsung hero you are in our family. When chaos and trouble are all around you, somehow you calm everyone. I thought for a while it was just me you were there for, but really it's been everyone. You helped Tavia work up the courage to do a back handspring in gymnastics. You beat up that guy who was dating both Gabby and Lona at the same time. You let my crazy mom be her normal, pushy self as you and Bianca planned your wedding, and, on that day, somehow you managed to thank her for it. Without a bit of hesitation, you're the first one to give my dad a hand when he's working out in the yard. It may seem like these are all small things, and maybe they are if you were related to us, but you do all this by choice. No matter how overwhelming the situation or how hard we Coglinaeses make it, you keep showing up and helping all of us.

"I don't know how my family will get through, this but I'm asking you to make sure they do. It won't happen all at once, and it won't be easy, but I know with you

there someone will always be watching out for my sisters. Someone will always be giving my dad a hand and graciously accepting my mother's unsolicited advice. Having four older sisters hasn't been easy, but it led me to the gift of having an older brother and is something I'll always be grateful for. Thank you for having my back. Thank you for helping me show them this is where I belong. And now, thank you for being there when I can't be. You are my brother."

I fold the paper back up and stuff it quickly into the envelope as though my overwhelming emotions might go with it. But they don't. I can't hold back the few tears blazing their way down my cheek and I can see that Bianca is having the same trouble.

"Damn you," she says, wiping at her eyes as she focuses on the road ahead of her.

"Bianca, I know he screwed up, but try to look at his motives. Look at all the years leading up to that, where he put up with all of our shit and stuck around. I know you're mad but—"

"Is he in danger?" She turns toward me and I see true concern in her eyes. "This stuff, whatever information he has, is it going to get him killed? I saw that cut over his eye."

"It's a big deal, but Jordan knows some people who can expose the information properly. She's offered the whole family her beach house in Florida while we work on it. She thinks something this big will be sweeping and made public, so the long-term danger will be minimal. "

"But there is short-term danger?"

"Yes."

She clamps her hand down on my forearm and squeezes it tightly. "You don't let anything happen to him. You protect him."

"I promise." I rest my hand over hers and pat it gently. "I'll make sure he comes home."

"I'm so glad that letter never had to be sent. I'm so glad you came home in one piece," Bianca says with a final sniffle.

"I'm not sure I am in one piece. It's really hard," I admit as I open my window and let the cool air dry the tears that formed in my eyes. "I thought I'd be one of the lucky ones who didn't come home and have trouble. But stuff like this," I gesture toward the letter before I tuck it away, "it's messing with my head."

"Go get some help," Bianca insists as she wipes away the last of her stray tears. "It's not something you should be doing on your own. I figured when you left Tennessee it was because you were struggling."

"I took a security job so I could feel like I was still doing something with a purpose. But even that didn't do what I needed it to."

"And what do you think you need?"

"I want to be able to be around you guys and feel good again. I don't right now. I came back because I knew one of you was in trouble. That's all Dad would tell me. If not for that, I'm not sure how long I'd have stayed away."

"And after all this is over, will you leave again."

"Probably."

"We're trying, you know. We don't know exactly what to do and we screw it up, but we love you," Bianca explains as she looks in the rearview mirror at her girls to make sure they are still occupied and not listening to this difficult conversation.

"I know you do. And it's not fair of me to expect you to have it figured out when I'm not sure what I need."

"Don't give up on us and we won't give up on you," Bianca says as she, for the first time since I've been back, cracks a smile.

"How the hell are we going to get Ma to agree to leave her house, her kitchen, and go to Florida? She's going to put up one hell of a fight."

"I'll handle Ma," Bianca says as her cool smile turns into a sinister one. "You just get the logistics planned and make sure this huge group of crazy people has a place to go and a way to get there."

"I feel like we should warn Florida. Maybe they can declare a state of emergency."

Chapter Seventeen

<u>Click</u>

"Can you all quiet down for a second?" Jonah pleads as he raises his hands to get the attention of everyone gathered at my parents' house. "I know this is not easy. We all have our lives and what I'm asking complicates things."

"I'm supposed to pull the kids out of school?" Tavia asks with a scowl.

"They're in preschool," Bianca interjects. "I think they can survive without playing blocks with their friends for a couple of days or a week."

"Their school is curriculum based and—"

"Shut up, Tavia. I swear if I have to hear about that damn school again I'm going to lose it. The bottom line is none of us are safe if we stay here. Jordan has been kind enough to offer us her family's beach house in Florida. We need to pack up and go," Bianca demands, leaving little room for debate.

"I have a job," Mick jeers arrogantly. "One where I keep my clothes on, so they really do expect me to show up every day." An audible low *uh-oh* rings across the room as Bianca takes a direct hit from him.

"You know what, Mick, you're right. You should stay. As a matter of fact, you should parade around town reminding everyone you're a part of this family. You can be the target," Bianca shoots back like she's striking him with a whip.

"Funny," he scoffs, making a teasing face back at her. To most people looking from the outside in, it would appear Mick is a jerk and Bianca hates him, but really this is just how we talk to each other sometimes.

I look over at my mother and see something more frightening than a full-on rage. Silence. Bianca clues into this, too, and she decides to poke the dragon.

"Ma, are you going to get your things together, or do you want to hang out with Mick here in Sturbridge?"

"I'm just at a loss, I truly am," she says, pursing her lips together and putting one hand up to her head as though she's about to faint. "In my generation it was always about family first." Her voice grows higher as she continues. "It was none of this nonsense of risking your life, especially when it means putting your loved ones in danger. It's a disgrace, really."

"If I can get on board with this plan after what Jonah and I have been through, then so can you, Ma." Bianca explains as she straightens her back, ready to argue her point.

"It doesn't sound like I have much choice. Everyone here is busy fighting everyone else's wars and can't make time for their own family." Like a petulant child my mother folds her arms across her chest and sinks her shoulders down.

"Oh stop it," Bianca says. She bends down to pat my father's golden retriever as though she can't even be bothered to give my mother all of her attention. "Don't act like it's just us being obstinate. You and Dad have never once sat back and watched something unjust happen. When you see something wrong in this world you do something about it. You always say something, Ma. As a matter of fact, that should be written on your tombstone: *She always said something*." Everyone in the room lets out a small, grumbling laugh before they force themselves to be angry or silent again. "You set that example and I know you're proud of Click and Jonah."

"I wish you wouldn't call him that," my mother sulks as she leans a little lower in her chair.

"That's who he is now. It's no different than me marrying Jonah and changing my last name. I grew up, found a new part of myself, and it changed parts of me. I don't see you insisting on me using my maiden name just because you gave it to me at birth." Damn, she's good. Why have I never thought of that argument before? "If you keep trying to turn him into the baby boy he was before he left for boot camp, you're going to lose the chance to know the really great man who's come back."

"He won't tell me anything, and now Jonah is doing something and he won't tell me anything either. He just left us." In my mother's normal fashion, she's somehow made Jonah's abandonment of his wife and kids about her, but Bianca doesn't take the bait.

"Sometimes people feel like they don't have a choice. Sometimes they think they're protecting you, or maybe they're protecting themselves." She turns her head around halfway so her eyes meet Jonah's for a brief second. In whatever language they've created between each other during their marriage, they exchange something that seems to resonate with both of them.

"I want to take my pans, all of them. And my bowls, the yellow ones from Tuscany. I'm not leaving them here," my mother insists as she gets to her feet and pulls me in for an unexpected hug. "Click, you go up to the attic and get our suitcases down while your dad gets Hemi ready to travel." I try not to get distracted by the news that the damn dog is going with them, and instead just soak in the seemingly small step my mother has taken toward accepting the changes in me. She finally called me Click.

"Come on, Hemi, let's get your crate ready," my dad says as he pats his legs and calls the dog over.

"Really, Dad, the dog is going too? I don't get this. You never liked dogs. Can't you board him or something?" I ask, and I know my level of frustration doesn't match the situation, but I'm so confused by this dog. She's sweet and all, and I've wanted a dog since I was a little boy, but it makes no sense now.

My father, whose face is usually pretty level, looks suddenly irritated. "She's a part of our family. If we're going, she's going."

"I'm just wondering why you put yourself through it. You're allergic. Even with the pills you're taking I can see she still bothers you." The room starts to clear out and, judging by the pace at which people are leaving, I can tell everyone knows something I don't. And it has them scattering.

"We're going to our house to gather up our things. We'll meet back here in an hour," Tommy says, and everyone nods in agreement and leaves just my father, Jordan, and me in the den.

"Keep an eye out for anyone or anything suspicious. Jonah has done a good job keeping clear of everyone here and we didn't have anyone tailing us today but still be cautious and get back here quickly," I instruct everyone as they make their way to the door.

"You've been really bugging me about this dog," my dad says, grabbing my attention again. "I think it's time we talk about it." The discomfort on my father's face has Jordan scrambling for a reason to leave, but she doesn't find one in time to get out. He's diving right in before she can escape. "I got Hemi about a month before your last tour was over. She was supposed to be a surprise."

"A surprise for who?" I ask, this still not sinking in.

"She's from Vets with Pets," my dad says as he scratches Hemi's ear. "She's trained specifically to help returning military personnel transition back home."

"What?" I ask, hearing his words but still not understanding. My father moves toward the desk in the corner of the room and opens up the drawer. Pulling out a stack of books, he drops them down on the coffee table in front of me. "Some people come home and they struggle with loud noises or crowds. Hemi is trained to alert and help you stay calm in those situations as well as navigate you safely away. I didn't know if you'd need her for those things, but I thought she'd be a good companion either way. A lot of the books suggest it."

I flop down onto the couch and start looking at the pile of books more closely. They're all about being a military family and how to support soldiers and returning veterans. There must be a dozen of them, and they're marked up with notes and highlighted passages.

"The dog was for me?" I ask, scratching at my head and looking up at him in disbelief. "Why didn't you tell me?"

"You weren't here long enough for us to talk about it. I thought I better just keep her until you were ready."

"When did you read all these books?"

"I've been reading them since you enlisted. Since we became a military family."

"A military family?" I know I sound like a jackass right now, but I can't believe the words coming out of his mouth. "You've barely said anything about me being a Marine over the years. You act like I was on vacation."

"I know," he admits as he takes a seat next to me. "Some of that is because I see how hard your mother is pushing you to talk about it and how uncomfortable it makes you. I guess I was trying to compensate for that. But I'm seeing now maybe there is some middle ground."

I shake my head in disbelief and look up at Jordan whose eyes are wet from impending tears. "The dog's for you," she says quietly.

"Thank you, Dad." I pull him in for a tight hug, slapping his back hard and never wanting to let go. I've thought for so long that his silence was from not caring about what I was doing. Now I feel my chest filling with emotion as I realize how much he really does care. How proud he is.

"Are you having any trouble, son? I've had the feeling you are, but I didn't want to confront you about it until you were ready to talk. The books say that. Do you think Hemi could help you?" The hopefulness in his eyes solidifies it for me. He really has been trying, and it makes me want to be honest with him.

"I've been having a little trouble. Maybe not stuff Hemi can help with, but when all this is settled with Jonah I think I'd like to spend some time with her."

"Vitty, do you want your blue suit or black suit?" my mother shouts down from upstairs, and the moment of calm connection evaporates as my father engages her craziness.

"Corinne, why on earth would I need a suit? You can't pack everything under the sun. We don't have time." He stands and hustles toward the stairs, ready to argue.

Jordan and I are left alone with Hemi, whose sweet face is staring up at me. "The dog is for me," I whisper as

I put my hand out and she obediently comes up under it with a light nudge.

"They really are trying." Jordan sits down next to me on the couch and I wrap my free arm around her. Hemi's big head flops down on my lap and her eyes turn up toward me.

"I better start trying too, then." I look into Jordan's face and wonder what the future might hold for me after all this is over with Jonah. I do think I need some help, but will I be brave enough to face that when the time comes?

Chapter Eighteen

<u>Jordan</u>

As a caravan of cars, weighed down by far too much luggage, pulled out of the driveway I felt a wave of relief wash over me. I've overseen dozens of multimillion dollar mergers and acquisitions yet the last hour of my life might go down as the most stressful to date. There were crying kids and people arguing over why some people had three suitcases but they only got one. Click's dad backed his car into Mick's car by accident and you'd think the small scratch was the same as totaling it.

"It's like the circus train pulling out," Jonah laughs as he waves a final goodbye to his daughters who are yelling out the window that they love him. He and Bianca didn't exchange many words but their brief hug before she got into the car spoke volumes.

"We need to get on the road ourselves. I didn't think it was a good idea to book flights to New York. If we drive we'll stay under the radar. Do you have your contacts lined up?" Click asks me as he keeps his eye on the tree line around us, looking like he's ready for something to strike.

"No. I'll have no problem getting face-time with these people. It's better if we keep our next move quiet."

"Do you know them that well?" Click inquires, and my face flushes a little. Again, if I were going to mention my history with Wes, now would be a great time. But I don't.

"First we need to pick up the flash drives from the places I've hidden them," Jonah says as he hops in the driver's seat of the car.

"I hope they'll be okay. I don't want to see any of them get hurt," Click says as we travel down the road in the opposite direction his entire family went.

"I'm sure none of this will impact them at all. We've got a good plan," I reassure him.

"I'm more worried they're going to kill each other," Click smirks. "The whole Coglinaese family stuck in a new place, living under one roof. It's going to be like a reality show down there."

"Hey Click, the closest flash drive is in a planter at Wheatley Market. You probably haven't been there since you were a kid. We can order those sandwiches we used to get. The ones with all the garlic," Jonah says with an excited smile.

"Great, I'll be stuck in the car with a couple of smelly guys for fourteen hours," I joke, but I stop short of laughing when I see the ominous look on Click's face.

"I can't go to that market. Skip that one and get the other flash drives." The blood has drained from his face and he's shaking his head, no.

"Why? You used to love it there. Plus it's the closest and most accessible one," Jonah argues, clearly missing the reason Click is asking for an alternative.

"It's an open air market with huge crowds and too much going on. I can't go there. It'll put me in a bad spot."

"What are you talking about?" Jonah asks, wrinkling his forehead as he tries to understand.

"I'm trying not to trigger too much stuff that bothers me. And that market will mess me up."

"Is this how you plan to live your life? Just avoiding everything that triggers bad memories for you?" Jonah's tone is harsher than I think necessary and it elicits the same response from Click.

"This from the guy who was on the verge of walking away from his entire life. You really want to have this argument."

"No, but I really want to get this flash drive, so you can stay in the car and I'll run in and get it. If you're good I'll bring you back a sandwich," Jonah jokes as he pulls the car into the busy parking lot of the market.

Click's right; it's busy here. The tents are all clumped together and people are walking shoulder to shoulder through the small aisles. I can imagine the anxiety this could bring on especially if he has a memory from an area like this where something happened.

"I'll go with you," I say as I unbuckle my seat belt and hop out of the car. "You're going to be digging around a planter, someone should be the lookout."

"No sandwiches," Click asserts. "Just the flash drive and come right back."

Jonah and I make our way through the market, weaving around the herds of people all loading their bags with vegetables, local honey, and crafts. He leads us to a slightly quieter area and takes a seat on a low brick wall that is full of green bushes with buds ready to bloom. Leaning back slightly he digs his hand into the dirt and pulls out a plastic bag and inside I can see the flash drive looking safe and intact.

"Shit," he gulps as he jumps to his feet. "That's one of the guys from my motel." He points to a lumpy faced man with broad shoulders and a scowl. He's about thirty yards from us but his glare is locked on Jonah.

"What do we do?" I ask, frozen for a second wondering if the number of people in this crowd is enough to keep us safe. Surely we can't get killed right here in public.

"Run," Jonah shouts as he clutches my arm and yanks me along behind him. I turn my head to see the man shoving people aside and breaking into a run himself. Jonah is hesitating to make sure I'm at his side but I charge forward, blowing past him. When he realizes I'm fully capable of maintaining this speed, he catches up and we haul ass back toward the car. I see Click standing against the side of the vehicle looking like he might throw up.

"Click," I yell, my breath nearly gone. "They're here." It's all I can muster but it's all he needs. I can hear the thudding steps of the man behind me getting closer and, as I look back to see how much distance I have between us, I stumble and slide forward, my palms and knees skidding painfully against the gravel. Jonah stops and turns toward me but I try to wave him off. "Go, don't let him get the drive," I demand as I try to get back to my feet quickly. Jonah ignores me and grabs me by the arm, lifting me in one fluid motion. But it's too late. I feel a handful of my hair along with the sleeve of my shirt get yanked backward as the lumpy faced man's hands clamp down on me. He pulls me to his body and wraps his enormous hairy arm around my neck. I kick him feverishly with my heel to his shin, but to no avail. I see Jonah pull the small clear bag from his pocket and hold it up so the man can see the flash drive inside.

"Take it," he says pleadingly. "Just let her go and you can have it."

"We know there's more," the man hisses and jerks my body slightly. "I'll trade her for you. That's it."

"Fine," Jonah says, raising his hands and walking toward us. "I'll go with you. I'll bring you to the copies I've made. Just let her go."

I expected more of a fight out of Jonah but maybe I've just been skewed from spending too much time with Click. Then I see it, Jonah's eyes flash with some kind of message for me that this is all under control.

As the large arm around my neck loosens I stumble forward and put my hands instantly to my throat, still gasping. I fall into Jonah's arms and try to tell him to run, that we could possibly get to the car and to Click but instead Jonah slides me behind him and as I peek around his shoulder I see the scene unfolding. Click has come up behind this man and puts him quickly in the exact same position he's just had me in.

"You like to choke women, huh?" he asks through gritted teeth as he bears down on the man, clenching his neck tighter and tighter until the man's body falls limp and Click releases him.

"Let's go," Jonah says, nudging me toward the car as I continue to hold my neck and try to right my breathing.

We spill into the car, my body shaking from my toes to my chattering lips. Jonah puts the car in reverse and skids out of the parking lot as Click turns around to look me over. When he sees the fear in my eyes he climbs over the center of the seats and drops down next to me in the back.

"I'm so sorry, that's my fault. I was so distracted by this damn place that I missed the guy tailing us." Click's face is wrought with guilt as he silently berates himself.

"I don't think he was tailing us. I guess thugs have to shop too sometimes. He had an arm full of bags that he dropped when he saw me. I think it was just a coincidence."

"I should have gone in there, not you. I'm so sorry," Click says again as he wraps his arms around me and I rest my head on his chest, letting the thumping of his heart remind me we're both still alive.

After a few silent minutes of driving, Jonah turns his eyes to the rearview mirror and looks at us. "Do we go get the next flash drive or just head for New York."

I feel slightly better now as I sit up and try to flatten my messy hair. "They know you're making a move now. All bets will be off. We need to get to New York and turn over what you have. We can make more copies."

Click nods his head in agreement and, though none of us are happy with only one flash drive in hand, we hit the highway for New York. I look down at my clothes and take note of how much I've changed since the last time I was in the city. I'd be almost unrecognizable at this point. Gone are my designer clothes. I haven't gotten a salon haircut in months and my nails are a mess. If I walked in for a mani and pedi at my old place now, they'd think I'd lost my mind.

The day I boarded a plane for Clover, North Carolina, I never thought would change me so deeply. Not just physically but emotionally as well. I never thought it would, in turn, lead me to Tennessee. I look over at Click. I am not the person I was before I met him. It makes my heart happy and, though my smile confuses him, he smiles back.

Chapter Nineteen

<u>Jordan</u>

"We can stay at my apartment," I say as I roll the stress out of my neck and try to stretch the ache out of my legs. Both Jonah and Click apparently have bladders the size of their whole bodies because the only stops we've made have been for gas, where they don't tend to have clean facilities for civilized ladies like me. Call me a snob, but I prefer my toilet to have a toilet seat and my toilet paper *not* to be a damp roll in the corner of a dirty bathroom. Still, I kept my mouth shut; the last thing any of us needs right now is an argument. I balanced on one foot and used some tissues from the bottom of my purse. As Click always says: improvise, adapt, and overcome . . . *pee accomplished.*

"You still have your apartment?" Click asks, sounding surprised although I thought for sure he already knew this. All the time we've spent together, all the talking we've done, there is clearly so much we haven't covered.

"Yes, I'm still paying rent on it. Now that I'm out of work I've had to stop the cleaning service from coming so it might not look great when we get there. It's small too, but I think we can make-do."

"Why did you keep your apartment?" Click asks in a low voice. "Is it in case things don't work out with us?" He is as uncomfortable and tired as I am, so I'm trying not to read too much into his tone.

"Do you know how hard it is to find a place in the city that's even remotely affordable? I'd be crazy to give it up. I wasn't sure where we'd end up, so I held onto it."

Jonah, reading the scene, jumps in. "I've never been to New York City. It's always been a dream of mine, but I never thought it would be for a reason like this."

"It's an incredible place," I say, beaming. "There is nowhere else in the world like it. Not that we're here on vacation or anything, but if there's time I'll show you some of my favorite places." This city holds a special place in my heart and I know I'm lighting up as I talk about it. I shouldn't feel bad about loving it, but for some reason it seems to be wounding Click the more I talk about it.

I reach out and lace my fingers with Click's, and although he doesn't completely reject me, there is a look of frustration on his face. I'm too tired to argue New York City rent controlled housing, so I start directing Jonah toward my place. I can see he's not used to driving in the city.

After the third time he brakes to let cars pull in front of him, I can't take it anymore. You're not supposed to use manners while driving here, you're supposed to use skill. "Pull over here; I'll drive the rest of the way. You're being too nice."

When we finally get to my place we've all pretty much stopped talking to each other. We grab our bags and lug them to the elevator and up to my loft apartment.

"It smells like piss in here," Jonah grumbles, lifting his feet up one at a time and looking underneath the soles of his shoes as though he might have stepped in a puddle.

"The whole city smells like that. You get to a point where you don't notice it anymore. I promise my apartment doesn't smell," I try to explain as I remember what it was like the first time I came to the city. It is really an assault on the senses. There's a constant clanking of metal and roaring engines of delivery trucks that don't look like they can fit down the congested roads. It's bumping shoulders with a hundred people on your walk to work every morning. Nearly getting hit by a taxi is a badge of honor here, and screaming the famous, "I'm walking here," as I slam my hand down on the front of the cab is a favorite hobby of mine.

I put my key in the door and turn it in that funny way I know I need to in order for it to open. Everything in New York City has these types of quirks. They infuriate most people but once you give into them, you fall in love with the city.

As I step in, my lungs fill with the smell of the place I've called home for almost a decade. I couldn't afford this place when I first got it, but I scaled back to eating yogurt and toast to be able to make ends meet. This place was the first thing I'd done completely on my own, and I knew if I could make it here I'd be able to survive anywhere.

"It's so small," Jonah remarks as he looks from one corner of the place to the other. It's a one bedroom, divided only by a partial wall. In reality, it's a glorified studio.

"Yep, but it's mine," I say flopping onto my couch. I've been away for so long and I know it's bad, but I have the urge to go hug all my designer clothes and sit out on my fire escape like I used to on hot nights. There is nothing in the world I've ever seen that compares to the skyline of New York City after the sun goes down. It's like the reverse of the night sky. All the lights are down here and the stars dull in comparison.

"So what's the plan?" Click asks uncomfortably as he takes only one step into the apartment and then freezes.

"It's four o'clock in the morning. We should all get some sleep and then Jordan can meet her contacts later on today," Jonah suggests as he tosses his bag down and makes himself at home.

"Cynthia Plante, Director of Deployment and Crisis Management at the EPA, is always in the office by five thirty in the morning. She's incredible. I'll get ready now and go see her first." I pull myself up off the couch and stretch my back.

"Are you sure? Maybe Jonah is right, maybe we should rest." Click is annoyed but finally trying to come a little farther into my apartment.

"You guys can stay here. I'll have better luck getting in there before the morning rush and having her full attention. She won't be pleased if I bring you with me." I don't dig deep enough into my own brain to decide if this is the real reason I'm not taking them or if I don't want to have to deal with Click and Wes being in the same room later in the day. I'm sure eventually they'll have to meet, but I'd like to have a chance to talk to them separately first. Even though I keep intentionally missing my chance to do that with Click.

"Do you think that's a good idea?" Jonah sits on the couch and pulls his shoes off, kicking his feet up on my coffee table.

"That's a one-of-a-kind bookmatched Cocobolo table. Can you get your sweaty socks off it please?"

"Oh, you're one of those," Jonah jokes, dropping his feet down and correcting his posture so that his back is straight as an arrow. "Is this better?"

"Much," I retort as I head into my bedroom and open my closet door. My clothes. My gorgeous, far too expensive designer clothes are, thankfully, all exactly where I left them. Heading to my tiny bathroom off my bedroom I spin the knobs to my shower and start to peel off my travel-worn clothes. I don't even remember where I got these jeans. Were they Rebecca's from my time in Clover? I had to borrow plenty of clothes from her when my pencil skirts and crisp white blouses couldn't accommodate the things we were doing there.

I step into the steamy hot water, my favorite part of this apartment, and let it burn my skin. The water heater knob broke two years ago and so the temperature can't be turned down, which is a blessing. I love a hot shower. It melts away every ache and worry, and for the ten minutes I stand beneath it I always feel peaceful.

Well, normally, but when I feel a hand reach in and brush my back I jump as though I'm about to be attacked by an axe murderer. "Sorry," Click says, pulling his hand back.

"It's okay, I'm just not used to having other people here. I forgot for a second." Again, though it's not my intention, my words seem to cause Click some kind of aggravation.

"How do you stand the water so hot?" He rolls up his sleeve and puts his arm on my back again and now I welcome the touch. If it weren't for Jonah I'd be pulling him in with all his clothes on and turning this into a much longer shower.

"It's not that hot," I lie, knowing the average person wouldn't enjoy this.

"It's turning your skin red. You could cook spaghetti in there."

I concede with a laugh and splash him with the steamy water. We haven't had any time alone in a couple days, and I'm dying to come out of this shower and get him naked and wet too.

"You know that's only half a wall," Jonah shouts from my living room. I close the shower curtain tightly, leaving Click on the other side.

"I'll be out in a few," I tell him, rushing through the rest of my shower routine, knowing my ability to keep my hands off Click will be better if I'm dressed.

After I'm out, a towel spun around my long hair to help it dry faster, I head back to my closet. There is no such thing as a walk-in closet in an apartment like this, but I've found every technique possible to maximize the space I have. I look through my outfits and pick one of my favorites. It's a crème-colored, draped frock jacket paired with a matching pencil skirt. Underneath I grab a plum bonded satin slip top that hugs my curves. I don't know what I'll encounter today, but I know how to dress in order to make sure I'm bringing all my assets to the table. There are days I'm not proud of using my sex appeal for persuasion, but at least this time it's for something good, not just to make more money.

I move to the bathroom and layer on an amount of makeup I haven't used since I left the city. I forget how polished it makes my skin feel and how my eyes pop when they are perfectly lined. My lashes double in length as I brush mascara across them. After a quick filing, I polish my fingernails and start sliding jewelry back onto my fingers, wrist, and neck. I've missed the sparkle. My push-up bra, combined with the rest of my magically slimming undergarments, makes my outfit look like it was tailored perfectly to my body.

I've almost forgotten how to do anything stylish to my hair. It takes me a few tries to get my large round brush moving in the right direction again. Finally, when everything else is primped and in place, I slide bright ruby-red lipstick across my lips and blot it against a tissue for the perfectly set look. Stepping back, I squeeze myself into the small space behind the door that allows me to see the full-length mirror. I slide on my far too expensive and much too tall high heels and look myself over. This is the Jordan I was for over a decade while working in the city, but for the last couple months this version of me has been buried.

As I step out of the bedroom I forget for a minute that, while this is what I looked like when Click and I met, that's not the case for Jonah.

"Holy shit," he gapes as he cranes his neck to look at me. "You look totally different."

"This is how I used to dress every day for work. Those weren't even really my clothes I've been wearing in Tennessee; I borrowed them from a friend in North Carolina where Click and I met."

"Yeah, this is her real life here," Click says as he flops down onto the couch next to Jonah and puts his feet up on the table I'd warned Jonah about earlier. But I don't bother asking him to put his feet down. I know he's trying to make a point. He's over tired and stressed and it's understandable.

"More like this was my old life. I don't plan to return to my old career, so I won't likely need any of this stuff or these clothes."

"What do you want to do now?" Jonah asks, tuning in to the tension between Click and me.

"I just want to help people. I don't know how or doing what." I twist my face, realizing I don't have many answers. "I don't know when either. I just know I want to do something that makes a difference."

"Then you two are perfect for each other," Jonah says, slapping Click on the leg and leaning back on the couch to prop his feet up again on the table.

"I'll call you after I meet with Cynthia and let you know how it goes. After her, I'm going to try to meet my contact at the FDA." Is omitting Wes's name intentional? I won't let myself answer that question.

"I still think I should go with you," Click offers, but I shake my head and wave him off.

"I'll be in touch all day. I promise." I walk over and plant a kiss on him. "You two take a nap," I break into a smile, "separately. You're grumpy."

It takes me a few extra minutes to calibrate my feet in these high heels as I navigate the streets I used to love walking. As much as I enjoy being back here I do miss the quiet I've learned to appreciate in the South.

The building that houses Cynthia's office is quiet this time of morning. I hope this works in my favor. I walk confidently past the front desk and security guard. He checks me out but doesn't ask me to stop. I learned a long time ago if you look like you know where you're going, people believe you belong there.

Getting by the front desk of the EPA's office won't be quite as easy. There is a pinched-faced, grumpy-looking receptionist who sees me coming and somehow manages to look even less happy than she did a moment earlier.

"I'm here to see Cynthia Plante, please," I relay with a wide smile that does nothing to soften the woman's demeanor.

"Ms. Plante doesn't schedule meetings this early in the morning."

"I know she doesn't, but I do know she's here. She's always here this early. If you could just tell her that Jordan Garcia is here to see her; I'm sure she'll make time for me."

"I'm sure she won't because she sees people by appointment only. If she didn't then anyone could walk off the street and come barging in."

"Well let's test your theory then. Nothing would make you feel better than calling back to her office and hearing her tell you to kick me out of here. So let's do that." With an angry grimace the woman picks up her phone and spins her chair around so I can't hear what she's saying. When her shoulders hunch slightly I know I've won. She turns her chair around and huffs out, "Go on back. She says you know where her office is."

"I do." I try to make my smile appreciative instead of gloating, but I don't think I'm successful. I weave my way through the large office, passing by dozens of closed doors with the lights off and head for the one woman who never seems to sleep. Her dedication is inspiring, and I hope she's willing to put some of that fierceness in the direction of this cause.

"Jordan," Cynthia says, clapping her hands together as she gets to her feet. "I haven't seen you in a while. Let me guess, your company has purchased an orphanage and wants to relocate it to a former uranium processing plant? You're here to ask me to look the other way?" She's always had a healthy appreciation for my directness even though we don't see eye to eye. Her sense of humor even in serious matters is endearing. Although our jobs have taken us in different directions, we've had a lot in common.

I toss my head back as I take the seat across from her desk. "Please tell me I was never that bad?"

"Was? Past tense? Did I miss something?" Cynthia's dark hair is in its usual tight bun and her almond-shaped eyes are lit up at the possible news.

"I'm currently unemployed. The last deal I was responsible for brokering was in Clover, North Carolina, and I didn't have what it took to crush a whole town of people once I found out how lovely they were. So I moved on."

"I'm sorry," Cynthia says, falling dramatically back into her chair as though the news has bowled her over. "This is like hearing the queen has been dethroned. I've never seen anyone as effective at her job as you were. You're the only person I know who always put in as many hours as I do. It's your company's loss, I guess."

"I'm sure there were ten people ready and waiting to take my job, any of whom wouldn't hesitate to do what's needed to make the company money. I was replaceable. To be honest though, I've never felt better in my life."

Cynthia looks at my face appraisingly as if she's carefully weighing my words. She's offered me a job a hundred times over the years. It's in her nature to help people, which is why working here is the perfect job for her. She makes people's lives better on a regular basis. "I'm glad. I'd love to see you start using your powers for good rather than evil. Let me know if you're interested in coming over to the good guys."

"I might take you up on that some day. But I'm here for something else today. It's of a sensitive nature. I've always known you to be a straight shooter. You are one of the most ethical people I've met, so I know I can trust you with this." I pull the flash drive out of my bag and place it on the table. "There is some very incriminating evidence here about thirteen tobacco processing plants that paid off federal officials in order to continue dumping waste. And that's just one infraction. The contamination is staggering, and I believe it's already impacting the surrounding communities."

"Jordan, these are very serious accusations. Are you confident in your source?"

"He's a long-time employee of one of the tobacco distributors involved. He's been threatened and physically attacked by people associated with the company in order to keep him quiet. I looked through the data quickly this morning myself. He's got photographs, internal memos, and banking information. This is the real deal."

Cynthia grabs the flash drive and plugs it into her computer. After a minute of clicking and keying a few things in, her mouth falls open. "Oh my word." Her face is as pale as her white silk shirt and her head is shaking in disbelief.

"I know," I say, my eyes matching hers in a look of incredulity. "My source is worried about his safety and that of his family. I'm hoping this can be addressed swiftly and the parties involved can be dealt with appropriately. The sooner that happens the safer they'll be."

"This would be the equivalent of the scandals in the early nineties that crippled these companies financially and put a lot of people in prison. Your contact is right to be worried about his safety. Last time something like this happened the whistle blower had death threats and his house was burned down. They'll do anything to keep this quiet."

"I've told no one I was coming here. You're the only one in the industry I've reached out to so far. If you're nervous about getting involved I can move on and not bring you into this," I assure Cynthia, knowing that question must be darting through her mind.

"Are you kidding me? Let's get these bastards."

"I knew you'd feel that way. That's why I told you first."

"But you plan to tell others?"

"Their infractions aren't limited to your jurisdiction."

"What else are we talking about here? I can hold off pursuing my angle if you need me to while you get the rest sorted out, but I can't hold this for long."

"I've got a contact with the FDA who I need to try to meet with next. I think I might need to involve the ATF because some of this might be considered trafficking of tobacco. I just don't have a contact there yet."

"I know someone but I'm not sure he'll meet directly with you. He's a little guarded, but very effective. I think he'd meet you if it were through me. It would be better if we get all agencies involved together first and come up with a game plan. I'll handle bringing in the ATF if you can get us a contact from someone at the FDA."

"A few more acronyms and we'll have the whole alphabet here," I joke, and Cynthia cracks a smile, though we both know how serious this is.

"When you're talking about something of this magnitude, people will act quickly, even if it is for self-serving purposes. Uncovering this type of scandal will garner *a lot* of media attention. If you'd come in here with less evidence or a smaller target it would likely take us weeks to get people willing to assist."

"I hope everyone agrees and this moves along as quickly as possible. I feel like the risk grows every minute.

"We can use my office as home base. Should we meet back here today? Maybe bring your contact too?"

"I think I can pull that off. Are you sure your ATF contact will come through that quickly?"

"We're . . . friendly with each other. If I call, he'll come."

"I'll have one other guy with me as well. Just so you are prepared," I warn Cynthia, not wanting Click's presence to be a surprise.

"What agency is he from?"

"The boyfriend agency. Well, the sort-of-fiancé agency, I guess. He's a Marine and he's invested in this situation as well. I didn't have him come this morning because I know it's hard enough getting a meeting with you when I show up alone."

"This has been a very interesting meeting so far. The Jordan Garcia I know would have been in here trying to get me to make a deal to protect these tobacco companies. She'd be robbing Peter to pay Paul and swapping information to get the company she was working for the best deal. And she certainly was never one to have a serious boyfriend, let alone a *sort of fiancé*. Whatever happened on that job down in Clover must have really hit you hard."

"It's been life altering, that's for sure. I've never been happier. It's weird, but getting dressed today and coming into the city . . . there are parts I miss, but really, I feel like I belong somewhere else. I just have to figure out exactly what my calling is."

"Well then, let's get this dealt with so you can get on your way. Whichever cause you choose to support or whatever people you get behind, they'll be lucky to have you."

My cheeks flush at Cynthia's kind words. "I'll see you back here this afternoon around four." I give her a quick wave and then pull my cell phone out of my pocket before I leave.

"Good luck at your next meeting," she offers and I stop in the doorway and roll my eyes.

"I'm going to need it. It's not going to go nearly as well as this one did."

"Why?" she asks, looking concerned at the stability of the plan.

"This went so well because you and I never dated. I can't say that for my next contact."

Her face softens and she waves me off. "Have fun with that. I'll see you later."

I pull up Click's number on my phone to update him but then reconsider. I hope he's asleep and shaking off whatever was bugging him. I don't want to interrupt, so instead I tuck my phone away and start heading to my next destination. Wiggling my toes in my high heels, I try to make them slightly more comfortable but to no avail. I'm out of practice. I talk myself out of taking a cab. I'm a New Yorker and it's only nine blocks. Most cabbies wouldn't take that fare anyway at this now busy time of morning.

Moving through the growing crowd of commuters, I head to Wes's office, feeling like I have a boulder in my stomach. Meeting with Cynthia was easy. We've met over drinks and swapped stories about what it's like to be a woman in this world. I have always considered her a friend. My history with Wes, on the other hand, is a bit more complicated. This could be interesting.

Chapter Twenty

Click

"Dude, you need to get some sleep. You only had a couple hours on the ride up here and it's making you pissy," Jonah tries to persuade me as he takes the remote from my hand and turns the television off. It doesn't matter; I wasn't watching it anyway. I'm too busy trying to get comfortable on Jordan's weirdly shaped designer recliner. Her entire place is one-of-a-kind or limited edition furniture. It's all worth more than anything I've ever sat on or next to in my life, so even though this chair has the softest leather I've ever touched, I'm having trouble relaxing.

"I'm not tired. That's not what's making me pissy," I reluctantly admit. Before all this happened I likely would have gone to Jonah without a moment's hesitation to talk about my problems. Things feel different now. I still don't agree with the way he left Bianca in the dark. It's hard when you realize the people you thought knew everything make the wrong choices.

"Let me guess, your girlfriend's old life is different than you realized and you're feeling insecure."

Damn, he's good. "Look at this place." I gesture around the apartment at every expensive detail. "How is she ever going to be happy with anything I can give her? This place is small but every square inch has something beautiful in it. Something very expensive. The nicest thing I own is a clean pair of boots I keep for special occasions. Did you see her today, dressed in those designer clothes? Maybe this is where she belongs. She certainly looked happy. I bet being back here has made her miss all of it. Tennessee, North Carolina, none of that is ever going to compare to the city for her."

"And what if she does want to come back? Can't you live here with her?"

"Can you see me living here? I couldn't even go into that crowded market yesterday. How would I deal with the noise and the chaos here? I've got enough stuff to process. This isn't the place for me to try to do it."

"Did she tell you she wanted to move back here?"

"Not in so many words, no. But I saw the difference in her when she got dressed this morning. She misses it; I can tell."

"Is that kind of like the way you miss being in the Marines? You and I have had this conversation a dozen times. Don't you miss lacing up your boots? Maybe she feels the same way about putting on her high heels. Don't you miss the camaraderie and the closeness? Maybe she feels that way about the people she used to work with. You miss the routine, maybe she does too."

"Shit," I mutter to myself, and I can see Jonah's face awash with understanding. I drop my head into my hands and groan.

"It's hard to notice when someone is feeling exactly like you are but for different reasons. This place, this city, was clearly a huge part of her life. It's who she was for a long time. Just because she still has some desire for it doesn't mean it's what she wants for herself anymore. It sounded more like she wants to do something new. Something to help people."

"It did sound like that, didn't it?" I rub my eyes and suck in a deep breath, now feeling angry with myself for not realizing how similar our situations really are. We both loved what we did. I think we were both very good at it. But just like I've given too much of myself to war, she seems to think she's given too much of herself to this lifestyle and is ready to find a new path, just like I am.

"Try not to assume too much about what she wants for her future. Just make sure you ask her flat out. She strikes me as the kind of woman who will tell you exactly how she feels."

"That's an understatement." I lean back in the chair and pull my phone out of my pocket. I expected her to call by now with an update. I know she's a very capable person, but I'm still starting to worry.

Chapter Twenty-One

<u>Jordan</u>

"Jordan Garcia," Wes greets me with a smile as he stands when I enter his enormous corner office with a view. He hasn't changed much since our last meeting although his suit seems nicer. His blond hair is still gelled straight back, keeping it clear of his blue eyes. He's got a boxy face that always made me think of the jocks from high school, a little Neanderthal. Wes wears his shirts too tight and his shoes are always a bit too shiny. The glare from them could blind you if they caught the sun just right. He was always a nice guy, but seemed to be trying a little too hard to be something he wasn't. It's one of the reasons I never saw a future for us.

What's different is the last time I was here he was working in a glorified broom closet I'm pretty sure didn't have a single window. He must be doing well.

"Hello Wes, thanks for seeing me on such short notice." He rounds his desk and pulls me into a hug, planting a kiss on my cheek. Not my normal business greeting, but he and I do have history. I'm just glad he's not still pissed at how I broke things off, or rather never broke things off.

"I'm surprised to hear from you since you never called me back. I have to admit, I was heartbroken." He puts on some pouting puppy dog eyes and, as I start to apologize, he stops me. "I'm kidding. I get it. We worked closely for a while and when that was over there wasn't enough left."

I'm shocked how synchronized we are on the situation. It makes me hopeful this will be easier to navigate than I thought.

"Judging by how many other girls you were dating at the same time, I'm guessing you bounced back quickly." It might have been too soon for the jab, but not long after I had stopped calling him, I had found out I was only one of a handful of girls Wes had been seeing at the time. That had lessened my guilt considerably.

"Ouch," he groans as he slaps his hand to his chest as though he'd just been shot. "That hurts, Jordan. You're right; those others were girls. And you're a woman. You're the one I really wanted."

My cheeks burn pink as his penetrating stare and attempt at smolderingly seductive eyes rake over me. He's standing too close for my liking, so I step back and take a seat in the chair across from his desk, hoping he'll go sit in his chair. He doesn't. Instead he leans against his desk so that his legs are open wide in front of me. Wes is an attractive guy, but now that I understand what love is really supposed to feel like, there is not an ounce of me that is turned on by him.

Wes straightens his cuff links and folds his arms across his chest, positioning them so his biceps look bigger than they are. How I ever read him as anything other than a self-centered snob, I don't know. But one thing that's indisputable is, he's very good at his job. I was certain of it before, having worked with him so closely but, judging by the new office, he's clearly still on that path. He was a bit of an underdog in this company, always seeming to be on the outside. That happens when you hold everyone to the letter of the law all the time. No one ever likes the compliance guys or the auditors charged with keeping everything in line. I'm actually happy that he's finally been recognized for his talents.

"It looks like you're doing really well here. You're great at your job so you deserve it. I knew you'd make your way up the ladder."

"Flattery will get you everywhere, Jordan. The last six months have been great for my career. It took a few key promotions. I've gotten away from the pharmaceutical side and now am working on more high-profile projects. I've got a hand in the studies of genetically modified foods and their labeling. You know that baby soap company that had formaldehyde in their shampoo? I helped rewrite the law that forced them to change their formula." I'm able to forgive the boastful look on Wes's boxy face because I'm genuinely impressed by the work he does. As I reevaluate my life, I like hearing the possibilities for actually doing some good in this world. I start to interrupt him but realize quickly he's not done. "I've got responsibilities with the CTP and even the Applied Nutrition Department. Since you dumped me I've really risen in the ranks."

I consider a witty retort about dumping him, but I'm too caught up on the details of his conceited explanation of his new job description. "The CTP, that's the Center for Tobacco Products, right?" I sit up a little straighter, waiting to see if I'm correct.

Wes looks slightly annoyed that I didn't take the bait about discussing the end of our relationship, but eventually he gives in and I get my answer. "Yes. The department was created in 2009 after the Family Smoking Prevention and Tobacco Control Act was signed into law. We set performance standards for tobacco products, keep advertising in line, and run studies on alternative products that could curb tobacco use."

"I can't believe this," I say with wide, excited eyes and a giant smile.

"Regretting your decision to break things off now, aren't you? I probably put your income to shame. There was a day you out-earned me by double. Not anymore."

I laugh and twist my face up, trying to see if he's actually being serious right now. I never considered his income a factor for dating him or, ultimately, not dating him anymore. "No, that's not what I'm excited about. It just makes what I'm here for right up your alley. I love when things work out like that."

Like a child whose hand has been slapped out of the cookie jar, I watch Wes's arrogant face crumple into a grimace.

He rights himself and shakes off the rejection. "Well it takes a lot of guts to come back here and beg me for a favor. You've always been bold like that. It's one of your many attractive features." I can hear his attempt at heat in his voice and now I'm so glad I didn't bring Click with me. Mostly because I know Wes enough to realize he'd be talking in exactly the same way, no matter what he knew about my relationship with Click. And that would have been disastrous.

"This is the kind of favor I think you'll like doing." I instantly regret my choice of words as a perverted smile spreads across Wes's face. "Not that kind of favor," I correct quickly, and he laughs. "I have some information here that could be a game changer. It's on track to be one of the biggest scandals for the tobacco industry in over a decade. I'm bringing it to you because I know you will handle it appropriately."

His face goes flat for a moment and then he swallows hard and stands. I don't care for the proximity of a certain piece of his anatomy in relation to my face, so I lean back even farther in my chair. Luckily he moves on quickly, walking to his door and closing it.

"Since when are you in the market of toppling companies and spearheading scandals? You've always been on the other side trying to keep this stuff quiet."

"We all change at some point. I've spent enough time on that side of it. I'm ready to do some good. Like you do." I'm pumping his ego now, because while I know he'll be lucky to have his name associated with this case, I still need him to drop what he's doing and come to Cynthia's office today, so I butter him up.

"Show me what you've got," he says, and I hand over a flash drive with a copy of Jonah's information. He rounds his desk and plugs it into his computer.

"There are hundreds of case studies and drug trials that have been tampered with by tobacco manufactures and distributers over the last two years. They've been trying to increase the reported side effects of drugs used to assist patients in smoking cessation. It's really quite brilliant. Maniacal, but brilliant."

"How did you get this information? Who's your contact?"

"He's solid," I answer, not ready to drop Jonah's name as it isn't really relevant anyway. I understand that Wes wants to make sure this is viable, but some details I intend to keep to myself as long as possible.

"Who else have you brought in on this, or am I the first? I can't be that lucky," he laughs as he scrolls through the information on his computer screen.

"I met with Cynthia Plante this morning. She's with the EPA. These companies have major environmental infractions that they've been paying to cover up as well. She's confident she can handle her side of this."

"Anyone else?" He's barely paying attention to me now as he taps his keyboard and digs into the data.

"No, just you, Cynthia and my contact." While I know there is a chance Cynthia is bringing in an ATF contact, I want Wes to feel like he's going to have point on this. If it helps him to feel like the most senior guy on this then I'll let him have that for now.

Leaving Click out of the equation is slightly more tactical though. Wes hasn't had a problem bringing up my history with him and I really don't want to go into the boyfriend conversation right now. I'm going to have to face this, but I'm uncharacteristically avoiding it. Damn you, heart for making things complicated.

"That's good. So what's the plan? I know you have one, you always do." There is sweat beading on Wes's forehead now, and he's looking slightly overwhelmed.

I smile slightly, remembering how strategic and effective I'd been at work and how much of a reputation that had earned me. "I know this is last minute but the plan is to meet at Cynthia's office at four this afternoon. We'll decide which bureau should handle which piece of the evidence and through which channels to pursue it."

"Okay. I'm glad you were smart enough to keep this quiet. The fewer people that know, the better it will be."

"It's not my first rodeo, though it's my first time on this side of it."

"I'm glad you came to me, but honestly I'm not sure why. How did you know you could trust me?" Wes leans back in his chair and folds his hands behind his head.

"Oh please, you never did me any favors. Even when we were dating you never even threw me a bone."

A devilish grin spreads across his face. "I tried throwing you plenty of bones, but you weren't interested in those." His eyes storm over and he laughs, but the smile disappears from his face in an eerie way. "I just find this so ironic that you're sitting there trying to play hero and I'm going to make sure this thing never sees the light of day."

I feel heat shoot across my chest as I try to process his words. I must have heard him wrong. "What are you talking about?"

"This," he remarks as he pulls the flash drive out of his computer and waves it at me. "No one is ever going to find out about any of this."

"Why?" A tremor in my hand starts and I glance back toward the closed door wondering if this is some kind of a joke.

"Because if they followed the trail it would lead right back here to me. Those idiots down South have been trying to run their game for years and we were always standing in their way. But that got me nowhere. Look at me now," he boasts as he props his feet up on his desk. Glancing down at his cell phone he taps at the screen for a moment, likely sending a message.

Blame it on the shock, but I'm doing nothing. I'm just waiting for him to break out laughing and tell me he's screwing with me. But every second that ticks by I can tell he's serious.

"That's only half of the proof," I blurt out, trying to think on my feet. "My contact, he's suspicious of everyone and wanted to hold the other half for security."

"Smart," Wes nods as a man steps aggressively into his office, closing the door tightly behind him. He's an angry looking beast of a guy and just the sight of him amps up my nerves even higher.

"What are you planning to do here, Wes?" I turn so that I can keep both these men in my peripheral vision at once. Not that I stand much of a chance defending myself against the ox-like man with the scar across his cheek.

"I'm going to go to that meeting at four this afternoon and let these secrets die with all of you."

"You're going to kill all of us? You're a murderer now?"

"No," Wes scoffs as he gets to his feet and comes around the desk toward me again. His hand comes to my cheek and he forces my chin up so that I'm looking right at him. "I'm a civilized human being. I don't murder people." He leans in and hisses into my ear, "I hire people to do it for me."

I slap his hand away and pull my face back in an angry fury. To my surprise, I feel the cold steel of a gun press against my temple. The scar-faced man is at my side and looking as if he'd love to do his job right now.

"Really, you don't think someone might hear it if you shoot me right here in your office?"

"I know a dozen other ways to kill you," the man grunts out. "And you wouldn't even have time to make a sound."

"We're moving the meeting. Call Cynthia and tell her your contact is spooked and we need to meet out on Clifton Avenue, behind the old factory there."

"I have to call my contact first. I haven't checked in all morning and he doesn't even know about the four o'clock meeting. I was going to call him after I left here."

"Just text him and let me read it first."

"He'll know something's wrong. I have to call."

"Oh, you're screwing him. I see. I was starting to think you were just a good old-fashioned cock tease." His hand is back on my jaw and this time, with the gun still pressed to my head, I don't slap him away. Not even as his hand trails down my neck and a single finger slips under the collar of my shirt.

"He's my boyfriend," I lie. "If I don't call him he'll know something's up and he'll take off with the other copies of the information."

"A real hero, huh?"

"It's what we agreed to."

"Fine. You call him first, but if I hear you tip him off I will have Leon here kill you. And I'll make sure it's not quick."

I pull out my phone and try to keep my hand from trembling. Now I wish I'd put everything else aside and had Click come with me today. He'd know what to do right now. I've got a plan in my head, but I have no clue if it will backfire. All I can hope is Jonah and Click catch on fast enough.

As the phone starts to ring I clear my throat and lean back so the gun isn't pressed directly against my head anymore. "I'm not going to be able to sound calm with that thing in my face," I whisper, and Leon drops it down to his side.

"Hello?" Jonah says, sounding a bit confused. Calling his phone rather than Click's is step one in my plan.

"Hey Jonah, honey, it's me. I've got to update you quickly, okay?"

"Okay," he says, still with a little confusion in his voice but at least he hasn't completely called me out.

"I have a meeting set up this afternoon at four with a couple contacts who are going to help us out. I'm going to text you the address where to meet. It's a little bit industrial and it's going to look off the grid a bit but don't worry. I'll text you the address.

"Okay," Jonah repeats. "How did everything go this morning? Where are you now?"

"I'm just leaving a meeting with my contact from the FDA." The gun is back at my temple as Wes leans down and puts his fingers to his lips, indicating I shouldn't say anything more about that.

"Babe, I need you to bring the second flash drive with the different information on it. I know you wanted to keep it safe and I told you that you could, but I was wrong. This is a really big case and I think you should bring it. We need all the firepower we can get."

"Umm . . . if you're sure," Jonah replies, and I'm so happy that he's not asking me what the hell I'm talking about.

"I'm sure. It'll work out, I promise. I'll send you the address now and then I'll call Cynthia Plante back at the EPA and let her know as well. Oh babe," I say, swallowing back my tears because I'm positive by now Jonah has switched his phone to speaker and that Click is listening intently. "Please let the dog out. I don't want him tearing up the house while we're gone."

"I will," Jonah says, and my heart jumps slightly as Wes gives me the hand signal to wrap it up.

"Okay, babe, I love you, I'll see you at four."

"I love you too," Jonah says without skipping a beat, and I disconnect the line.

"Love, really? Jordan Garcia is in love. Well I guess the whole world is upside down, isn't it? Straight shooter Wes is now playing ball with the bad guys and Jordan is head over heels for a whistle blower." Wes is talking in an almost frantic tone that tells me his nerves are ragged and he likely is in over his head here. "Call Cynthia and give her the new meeting place. Text it to your little boyfriend too. Then give your phone to Leon so he can trash it. I don't want anyone tracing you between now and then."

"I don't understand why you'd do this, Wes. You were such a staunch believer in what you were doing. You loved protecting people."

"And it got me absolutely nowhere. The only way to get ahead in this world is to align yourself with the people who have the money and the power. Fighting them does you no good. You and your little boyfriend are about to find that out firsthand."

"Why even bring her to the meeting? We can get rid of her now," the scar-faced man grunts.

"Since when do you give orders?" Wes asks indignantly. "I want to see these two lovebirds together. Let's not rob them of that." Wes lets out another hardy laugh and Leon shrugs his agreement as he tucks his gun back into his belt.

"Get a couple other guys ready to go with us. I don't want any mistakes here. We need to bury this, and all of them, tonight." Wes turns toward me and leans in close. "I have no intention of giving up everything I've earned just because your little boyfriend got nosy."

Chapter Twenty-Two

<u>Click</u>

"Shit," Jonah says as he runs his hands through his hair. "At first I was like, what the hell is she talking about, but then I could tell. Something wasn't right. Did you tell her the damn hostage word? The dog. That's what she was talking about right?"

"Yes," I say flatly as I continue to strap weapons to my body and then lace up my boots. "We need to find her and fast. I don't want to wait until the meeting time. I've got a system on my phone that can track her cell but hers has been shut off. So we'll have to go off the clues she was trying to give us."

"What clues?"

"She told us she met with Cynthia Plante from the EPA. We can start there."

"Click," Jonah says as he catches my arm, trying to get me to slow down. "Who could have her? These guys in Tennessee—there is no way they could have linked her to me so quickly and tracked her down in the middle of the city."

"You're right. If they had, they'd likely have come here to her apartment first. So my guess is one of her contacts wasn't as trustworthy as she thought. Maybe they didn't like what they were hearing and it went south. But since we don't know who she was meeting with today we can't really help her that way. The best we can do is retrace her steps and hope Cynthia knows who she was supposed to see next."

"I should have asked her more questions on the phone. I'm sorry. I just wasn't sure what she was trying to say."

"You did perfect, actually. Asking more questions could have put her in a lot of danger. You played along and let her get out as much information as she could." I slap him on the shoulder and open the door. Slinging my bag over my shoulder I look back at Jordan's apartment one more time and try to reassure myself we'll all be back here together in no time.

"I need you to start making phone calls or check the Internet. We need to find out where Cynthia's office is and fast," I instruct Jonah.

"Even if we find it, she might not want to meet with us."

"I don't plan on asking nicely more than once. She'll meet with us." I know, to Jonah right now, I'm sounding flat and disconnected. I should be freaking out and losing my mind because the woman I love may be in mortal danger. I've been trained and battle tested to make sure in the moments when everyone else is falling apart, I'm keeping it together. It's how lives are saved. Emotion will still be there, but it serves me almost no purpose right now. I can't cry Jordan back home. I can't wish her back home. I have to go find her and fight our way back home.

After just a few minutes and a couple phone calls, Jonah has located Cynthia Plante's office and we start making our way there. After a harrowing twenty minutes of navigating this city I'm leaning over the receptionist's desk and speaking in a level tone as I ask to see Cynthia.

"Sorry," she says, spinning a coil of her hair flirtatiously around her finger. "Ms. Plante doesn't see anyone without an appointment. She's in with someone right now anyway and she's asked me not to interrupt."

"This is an emergency," I plead.

"Everyone says that." She's batting her eyelashes coyly at me and it's just annoying the hell out of me.

"If you tell her I'm here she'll see me."

"You're the second person today to tell me that. I think I know Ms. Plante well enough. I know how to do my job."

"Who was the first to say that today? Jordan Garcia?"

The receptionist's face goes flat and I know I'm right. "Jordan is in danger and so is Cynthia. So nothing is going to keep me from getting to her office. Point me in the right direction please."

"I can't. I'm going to have to call security," she says as she reaches for her phone.

I nod my head at Jonah and walk past the receptionist's desk and ignore her demands for us to stop. After I walk far enough away to drown out her voice, I poke my head into the first office. "I'm so sorry to bother you but I'm a bit lost. Can you direct me to Cynthia Plante's office?"

The plump woman smiles and nods as she steps out in front of me and directs me through the maze toward Cynthia's office.

"Thank you," I smile, and I walk right into Cynthia's office, interrupting her and the man sitting across from her desk. The man has a crew cut and a badge hooked on his belt. His pock-marked face and angry scowl lets me know he's not happy for the interruption.

"Cynthia Plante?" I ask, and her eyes turn immediately to the man in the chair across from her.

"Who are you?" he asks, standing and resting his hand over the weapon on his hip.

"My name is Click, I'm Jordan Garcia's boyfriend, well fiancé, sort of. Was she here this morning?"

"Don't answer that, Cynthia. If you don't know this guy then we don't know who he's working for," the man with the badge commands.

As the man starts toward me I hear the clattering of more people behind me. Security has arrived to escort us out. "Wait," I say, raising my hands, trying to look like less of a threat and speaking to who I hope is the most level-headed person in this room. The only one who doesn't get paid to kick people out or keep order.

"Cynthia, please, Jordan is in trouble. Wherever she went when she left here, something went wrong. She needs our help but I can't find her without getting more information from you. Please," I beg.

Cynthia looks at each man in the room and raises her hand for everyone to wait a moment. "Tell me something about Jordan that lets me know you are really her boyfriend."

"She's a pain in the ass," I blurt out. "She is stubborn and at first glance you'd think she was not at all worth the trouble, but once you get to know her and you see her heart the way I did when I met her in Clover, you know she's worth every bit of trouble."

Cynthia's nervous face settles into a small smile as she waves off security and invites Jonah and me to join her. "This is Deputy Director Bill Gully from the ATF. I was just briefing him on the information Jordan provided me this morning. Now tell me what's going on with Jordan."

"She called and used the hostage word we'd discussed. I believe whoever she met with after you may not have liked the information she had, could possibly even be involved, and is keeping her against her will."

"That's why they moved the meeting," Bill says, leaning in toward Cynthia and keeping his voice low.

"It's at an industrial area now, right?" I interject and step into the office even farther. "I think it's a setup. They are likely trying to silence this and will be fully able to if they can get everyone who's involved in one secluded place at the same time."

"Wait, what are you suggesting?" Cynthia asks, her nostrils flaring. "You think they want to kill us?"

"Yes," I say flatly, not wanting to soften the news.

Cynthia's eyes fix back on Bill's as she trembles slightly. "Don't worry, Cynthia, I'll take care of it. You won't have to come within ten miles of that meeting," Bill assures as he pulls out his phone and gets ready to dial.

"I think I know where she was going when she left here. Who might have been her next contact," Cynthia squeaks out, still looking scared. "It was an ex of hers. Someone she dated. I don't know his name but I know someone who might; hang on." Cynthia picks up her phone and makes a call to someone and speaks frantically but quietly. When she hangs up, she looks up at us. "That was a mutual friend of ours. She remembers her dating someone in that office named Wes, but she doesn't know his last name."

"That's great, Cynthia," Bill assures, reaching over and patting her arm. "That'll help tremendously."

"What's your plan?" I cut in before Bill can try again to queue up a number on his phone. I don't let the new information that this person holding Jordan might be an ex-boyfriend of hers bother me. It changes nothing. Danger is danger.

"I'm going to get the closest tactical team briefed and set up at the location. I'll get as much information on Wes as possible and try to have someone get eyes on him now. If that doesn't resolve the situation and the meeting has to take place I'll have an agent pose as Cynthia. I'm guessing this guy is the contact they're trying to get their hands on?" Bill asks, gesturing at Jonah who's been silent until this point.

"Yes sir," he says, nodding his head.

"I'll stand in as him. I want to be there," I demand and ready myself to have to fight for that.

"And who exactly are you?"

"I'm a Marine, former Special Forces. I've been involved in numerous hostage situations including extractions from hostile zones. I'm combat trained and I can be an asset. I've given six years of my life to this country and all I'm asking is for a chance to use what I've learned to save someone I love."

"You have absolutely no authority or jurisdiction in the matter. Not to mention you've got skin in the game. She's your girlfriend. I don't need that kind of emotion clouding things up," Bill fires back.

"I can assure you emotion will play no part in my ability to assist. You need me."

Bill lets out a dismissive laugh, "And why is that?"

"Hostage situations turn out significantly better if the person being held can remain calm. If Jordan sees me she'll be calmer than if she sees strangers. Plus you have under two hours to get a tactical team in place and briefed. Getting an agent up to speed on the situation and the nuances of the background here will take time you don't have. No one is closer to this scenario than I am."

The arrogance fades from Bill's face and he clears his throat, giving my words some thought. "You can ride with me and discuss your previous experience and how ready you really are for this. I'm going to have your records pulled and see if everything checks out. If I hear what I need to I'll let you stand in. But there will be a Tac Ops leader there, and you will take all your orders from him. This is not a one-man mission."

"I know how to take orders, sir. I've been doing it for the last six years. You have my word."

"Wait," Cynthia calls out as we stand and head for the door.

"Oh, Cynthia, I almost forgot. I'll have agents here within the next few minutes and they'll stay with you until this is over. You'll be safe. I promise I won't let anything happen to you," Bill assures, and in an instant I realize why he's so motivated to help. He's jumped into action quicker than I expected and, while I'm grateful for it, I was skeptical. Now I see he, too, has some skin in the game.

"Thank you, but that's not why I stopped you. Click, I've been working in the same circles as Jordan for almost a decade. We started out around the same time. I just wanted you to know that she told me today she's never been happier. I've never heard her talk about anyone or any part of her life like that. She loves you very much and she called herself your fiancée. I just wanted you to know."

"Thank you," I say in just above a whisper as I avert my eyes and move Jonah, who seems slightly in shock, so we can head for the door.

Chapter Twenty-Three

<u>Click</u>

Bill is still on the phone ordering everyone around and getting things set up. He's curt but effective and I'm glad he's at the helm of this. Jonah and I are in the back seat of his car as he speeds through the intersections, sending us sliding back and forth.

"We need to swap clothes," I instruct Jonah as I start pulling my T-shirt over my head. Bill tosses a bulletproof vest over the seat at me and I start strapping it on.

"Why are we changing clothes?" Jonah asks skeptically.

"Because I need to look more," I wave my hand at him, "boring I guess."

"This is a nice shirt. Bianca got this for me for Christmas." He looks down at the blue and gray striped collared shirt and then his khakis. "Fine," he says, seeming to reluctantly agree that his clothes are different enough from mine to make a difference in this.

As we swap the rest of our clothes, I pull the letter from my bag. I look down at it and hesitate before handing it over. "I wrote this when I was deployed. It's had your name on it a long time. It's part of the reason Bianca decided not to kill you. I showed it to her when we were driving over to my parents' house to send them off to Florida."

"What's it say?" He looks nervous as he hesitantly takes it from my hand.

"It's just something to hold onto if anything should happen to me. I thought once I was home I wouldn't need it anymore, but who am I kidding? I wouldn't be happy unless I was in some kind of danger." I try to lighten the moment, but Jonah ignores my humor. He tucks the letter into his pocket.

"I'll be giving that back to you today," he assures me as he laces up the boots I just shoved over to him. "How do you wear these things? They are so damn heavy."

"I was just going to ask how you wear these sneakers. They're so damn ugly."

He laughs but it's cut short as Bill starts shouting loudly into his phone. Jonah leans over toward me. "You sure you can do this? With the flashbacks and stuff, do you think you are okay for this? You told me what happened after your car accident. What if something like that happens today?"

"I'm fine." I throw him a sideways look that tells him to drop it, and he does. "I can handle this."

"Son," Bill says, and his round black eyes catch mine in the rearview mirror. "Tell me how you think this is going to play out. You know the players to some extent, and you know what's at stake. How do you see this going?"

I can tell by the penetrating look he's giving me this is a loaded question. My answer will likely decide my readiness for this operation. Sure, he's already tossed me a bulletproof vest, but that doesn't mean he's given me the green light yet.

"Best case scenario is they don't know we've been tipped off. They'll be expecting an unarmed EPA agent and a civilian. Our best hope is they are arrogantly underprepared."

"And the hostage, Jordan?" Bill asks in a leading tone.

I turn my head so I'm looking directly into Bill's eyes and Jonah is outside of my peripheral vision. I don't want to see even the flinch in his reaction. "She's probably not going to be there. She's likely dead already."

"Click!" Jonah's voice is sharp and high, but I still don't turn toward him. "Don't think that," he insists.

"If these people are plotting to kill anyone involved in this in order to keep it quiet, they wouldn't bother keeping her alive. By setting up the meeting and getting everyone else with knowledge in one secluded place, she'd have done all they required of her. She doesn't serve any other purpose to them," I say flatly, trying not to let an ounce of emotion show through.

"That's true," Bill agrees. "But there is a small chance if they are worried about the other two people due at the meeting spooking they'll bring her along. If they are desperate to end this tonight they'll want to make sure everyone who should be there shows up, and having Jordan alive and present could help with that. But I agree, the odds of that are low. I was just wondering if you'd considered that."

"I've considered everything, sir. If Jordan isn't on the scene, or even alive anymore, the best chance at bringing those involved to justice will be at that meeting today."

"Are we clear on what the word *justice* means, Marine?" Bill asks with a cocked eyebrow and a stern glare.

"I'm no vigilante. Trust me. If I were going to take the law into my own hands I've had dozens of opportunities before this. I know my place today." The words I'm saying are true but my conviction behind them feels hollow. While it's true I've never crossed that line before, I feel less confident I won't today. If I find they've hurt or killed Jordan, I won't let a single one of them survive. And there won't be anyone in the world capable of stopping me.

"This is where you two part ways then. ATF agent Maggie Dorado is about to step into the car and you, Jonah, are about to step out. Maggie will be posing as Cynthia at the meeting. Jonah, another officer will escort you somewhere safe and you'll be kept apprised as things unfold.

"Thank you, sir," Jonah says, reaching up to the front seat and shaking his hand. "Keep my brother safe please." He nods his head toward me and then opens his door to step out.

Bill looks over at Jonah, and though it seems against his better judgment, he says, "You'll be with Cynthia. I . . ." He looks away awkwardly. "I've always kind of had a thing for her and intend to ask her out on a proper date when this is over."

"I'll keep her safe," Jonah assures but he is cut off abruptly by Bill's husky laugh.

"That's not what I was saying. She'll have plenty of agents there to do that for both of you. I'm just letting you know to keep your hands off. She's mine."

Before Jonah can explain he's a married man, Bill is speeding away and I have to lunge across the back seat to grab the door Jonah didn't have time to shut. As we fly around a corner, the door I just slammed closed is quickly pulled back open. Hopping into the seat is a woman in her late twenties with raven-colored hair that is pulled back in the same fashion Cynthia's was. She's wearing a similar style suit. I watch as she slips out of her flat shoes and into a pair of high heels.

"This is my least favorite part of today so far," she huffs. "How the hell am I supposed to do my job on these stilts?"

"You'll be fine. You have your vest on?" Bill asks as he speeds around another corner.

"Of course."

"Good, now you two get yourselves calibrated on the assignment. You'll be out there on your own for the most part. I'll have agents with eyes on you from various locations, ready to act if needed. But ultimately it will be on you two."

"Yes sir," Maggie and I both say in unison. As I start to brief her on who I am, and what else I know about the situation, I push out all the thoughts I have on Jordan and what must be going through her mind right now, if she's alive. None of that will help me save her, so I lock it away.

Chapter Twenty-Four

<u>Jordan</u>

I should be terrified, but all I can muster right now is anger. I'm pissed, mostly at myself for the poor judgment in coming to Wes and how that might impact everyone else involved. While I'm confident my message was received by Jonah and Click, I don't know what they'll be able to do to protect themselves and Cynthia at this meeting.

There are now four thugs in the SUV I've been thrown into, and I mean that quite literally. I've got the ache in my ribs where I collided with the console as proof of how little they care what happens to me. The man driving is of some Russian descent and he's the angriest looking of all of them. I'm alone in the third row seat, my hands restrained with duct tape. They pull the truck into a gas station and I hear them arguing about who was supposed to fill it up before they left. The driver gets out and I pull my body up slightly to see the gas station is lively and full of people. If I were going to make a move and have any chance at escape it would have to be now.

I'm the only bargaining chip they have. If I can get away there will be no need for the meeting. We can expose the information we have and take them all down. This is what is making me so pissed right now. I'm the only one who has put all of us in jeopardy.

The other men all step out of the car. Two go into the gas station and one walks off to light a cigarette. I can see the SUV doors are unlocked. They've given me no credit since the moment they captured me and maybe they are right not to, but I'm still going to try. I heave my body over the seat and back myself up to the door away from the man pumping the gas. I position my hands around the handle and pull it open. I tumble backward onto the hard cement but my adrenaline is pumping too hard for the pain to slow me down. I roll to my side and get awkwardly to my feet. I consider screaming, but as I look around I see a woman pushing a stroller and I'm too afraid these men will indiscriminately fire just to kill me. I couldn't live with myself if anyone was killed in the crossfire. Instead I kick off my sky-high heels and take off running, charging as fast as my legs will take me away from the gas station.

My eyes are locked on the small strip mall across the street and I keep telling myself if I can get there I'll be fine. There will be endless places to hide. I just have to get there. As I dart across the street, cars squealing their brakes to avoid me, I see him. Wes jumps out of his sleek black Mercedes and he's at my side before I can outrun him. His hand is tight on my arms, still secured by tape, and with no other choice now, I start screaming. Though every eye is on me, no one is making a move to free me from Wes's tight grip as he drags me back toward his car. Although I kick and swing my head wildly, trying to get away, he proves too strong for me. Pushing me through the driver's side door, he shoves my body until I'm in the passenger seat.

"You always have to put up a fight don't you, Jordan?" he accuses as he wipes the blood from a scratch I've left on his cheek just below his eyes. "I don't want to hurt you but you're giving me no choice."

"You don't want to hurt me, but you're going to kill me," I spit back as I try to unlock the door and get out. I'm not sure why I didn't expect it since Wes seems to be in a position where he will stop at nothing, but when he throws the first punch at me I'm still shocked. It lands off target, striking my shoulder but it's so powerful I can't breathe for a moment. I duck my head the best I can, but without the use of my hands and arms, I am unable to shield my face from his repeated blows. As he slams the car into drive I get a small reprieve from his pummeling, but it isn't until I slouch over, my body limp as I give up, that he finally stops.

My ears are ringing, and I know the skin above my eye is cut. The partially healed cut on my forehead from the accident feels like it may have opened back up. I can taste my own blood from my split lip. I close my eyes and lean my head against the window, feeling my head slip a little as my blood makes the glass slick.

Wes has his phone to his ear, and though I'm dazed, I try as hard as I can to tune into his words. "You fucking idiots. You are so lucky I was behind you and saw her get out of the car. I gave you one job and between the four of you she still got away." He pauses while they try to explain but quickly cuts back in. "Yeah, trust me she's under control now. She won't be getting away again. I pay you so I don't have to do this kind of stuff. You know I don't want to get my hands dirty in all this. Beating the shit out of girls is not my thing. Just get your asses to the meeting place. I want you to be there early. You need to get the jump on them. Now I'm wondering if you guys can even get this done. Can you kill these people or what? I'll be close by watching." He pauses again, listening to the person on the other end of the phone. "I don't care if you said I should have already killed her and this wouldn't have happened. It's my call when we get rid of her. I'm not done with her yet." He hangs up the phone and tosses it heavily into the cup holder. I feel his hand slap down on my thigh and part my legs but I'm too overcome with pain to stop him. "I'm not done with you yet. You and I have some unfinished business. I invested a couple months and some expensive dates on you and I want what I paid for," he hisses as he slams my leg closed and puts his hand back on the steering wheel.

A couple of stray tears roll down my face as I finally begin to realize how much trouble I might be in here. I don't doubt for a second that Click is working, doing something, to try to get me back. But the chances are growing slimmer he'll be successful at this point. And if Wes makes good on his innuendo, even if Click does save me, will I ever be the same?

Chapter Twenty-Five

Click

I'm relieved to know Maggie is qualified and incredibly competent and I don't doubt if this goes south she's equipped to hold her own. That's always a good feeling when entering these situations. You want to know you've got a good team. We've gotten word the site seems clear and the tactical team is in place. They've got eyes and ears all over the place and both Maggie and I are wired into their frequency. We can hear them and they can hear us. The code word for alerting them to take the shot is *cavalry*. I'm hoping it won't come to that, but I'm too realistic to believe it won't.

I've got my weapon in a cross draw holster. Safety off, one in the chamber, and ready for anything. Maggie and I split up, both hopping into the cars the ATF has set up for us and driving the couple blocks toward the meeting site. I hear the tactical team updating us on what they see. A black SUV has just pulled in and, though the windows are tinted, through infrared scopes they've identified four people inside. No other cars have come to the large parking lot since the team has set up. It looks like this might be the only obstacle for us. If Jordan is one of the people in the SUV then Maggie and I are only outnumbered by one. That's manageable.

I hear Maggie's voice come through the small speaker in my ear and she sounds as confident as I'm feeling. "Just one SUV. That's too bad, I thought we'd actually have a challenge here today."

"I'm pulling in now," I say as I turn into the opening in the chain link fence that leads behind the mill. "I've got eyes on the SUV."

"Right behind you, Click," Maggie responds, and I see her car pulling down the road behind me. I pull up, parking strategically so the car is between me and the SUV for a layer of protection. The driver steps out of the SUV just as Maggie is pulling up. He's a monster of a guy with a tattoo that creeps over the top of his shirt and up his neck.

"Pretty cool spot to meet," I say in a bit of a goofy voice as I look around as though I'm thoroughly impressed.

The man who now stands by the driver's side door of the SUV grunts, and I can tell he's not going to be playing the part of someone who is meant to be at this meeting. He's not making an effort to make me comfortable or convince me everything is all right. That means the only thing he is waiting for is Maggie to step out of the car so he can kill us both. Realizing there are likely multiple guns pointed at me from behind the tinted windows of the SUV, I turn and jog casually back toward Maggie's car. "This must be Cynthia," I say over my shoulder to the man, as if he'll give a shit.

When my back is turned on them I speak so the tactical team can hear me. "Cavalry, repeat cavalry. They're not putting on a show here. Once they have a clear shot at us they'll be ending this. They'll want the second half of the flash drive Jordan told them about, but they don't need us both alive to get that."

In my ear I hear the Tac Ops leader, Frank, speaking. "I've got a clear shot to the man outside the SUV but without knowing if there are hostages inside I can't take shots at the vehicle. You'll need to assess that and handle it on the ground. If they step out and we identify them as threats they will be neutralized from up here."

"Copy that," Maggie says, but I don't respond. I open her car door and she steps out with a fake smile. "I go left, you go right," she orders quietly, and I nod my head in agreement.

"The assailant outside the SUV has pulled a weapon. It's down by his side but it looks like he intends to fire once you're both back in sight."

"Copy," Maggie responds again. We're separated from these men only by thirty feet and the cover of my strategically parked car. "I'll bait him," Maggie says as she reaches behind her back casually and hollers at the men. "Was it really necessary to meet all the way out here? This seems absurd."

At that, the man raises his weapon and she and I hit the deck behind my car as the bullets rain over our heads. I hear a heavy grunt and a body falling to the ground as Frank's voice rings in my ear again. "Assailant one is down. Multiple people are exiting the car. I count three. All armed and taking cover behind the SUV. We're waiting for clear shots."

I don't need more than a second to do the math. If there are four armed men who have come out of the SUV then that accounts for all the heat picked up on the infrared scopes. And that means Jordan isn't there. That hits me right before I regain my emotional footing. Both Maggie and I have our weapons drawn, waiting for more direction from the tactical team. More bullets fly out over our heads and I go belly down to get a view under my car and, in turn, under the SUV. I see a set of boots and with a steady hand I fire, directly hitting one and watching the man fall to the ground. With another shot to his recently dropped body I see him go still.

"Was that you guys?" Frank asks, and I confirm the shot was mine. "Nice work. Two targets left and my team is getting in place to take them out."

"Leave one alive," I demand. "The hostage isn't here and if you kill them all we may never find her."

"I'll order a non-fatal shot, but it'll be up to you to disarm him and secure the scene," Frank offers and I accept the challenge. Judging by the fiery look in Maggie's eye, she's game, too.

After a minute we hear Tom's voice one more time. "Two remaining targets are down. Injured but moving. I cannot confirm if they are disarmed. Approach with caution."

"I'm with you, Click, but if we get around that corner and it's them or us, I'm firing."

"I go left, you go right. Let's try to keep one of them alive." I let her see the look of desperation on my face, just for a flash.

We're on our feet and splitting up as we round the corner of the SUV. One man, bald-headed and dressed in a suit, raises his gun and, despite Maggie's orders for him to drop it, he sends off a round that nearly hits her. She shoots him directly between the eyes. At the sight of this, the last man drops his gun and sends his hands high into the air in surrender. I'm on top of him in a flash. I flip him over and secure his arms as I hear the charging footsteps of the tactical team around us. Maggie is kicking the weapons out of reach even though the remaining men are dead.

"Check the SUV," I beg her, and as the rest of the team approaches she does. Thirty seconds later she's hopping out with a somber look on her face. The only thing worse than Jordan not being in there would be if she was but not letting off any heat to be picked up by the infrared scopes. She'd be dead.

"Clear," Maggie tells the tactical team and then turns toward me. "She's not in there."

I grab the man by the collar, lift him, and then slam him down. "Where is she?"

"Go to hell," he shouts back as he spits out the dirt that's just been crammed into his mouth. "Arrest me, I don't give a shit."

I pull my weapon and press it to his head. "I'm not a cop. I'm her fiancé. Tell me where she is or I will give you a matching hole in your head." I gesture over to his dead buddy lying next to us.

Two of the tactical operations team members point their weapons at me but Maggie orders them down. "Let him do it," she shouts and the man looks up at her like she's crazy. Like we're all crazy.

As the men lower their guns I cock mine so that he knows I'm serious. At this point, I really am. "Wes has her. He was keeping her alive for his own reasons. I don't know what."

"Where is he?" I shout, slamming him down into the ground again.

"I don't know. He said he'd be close. He was watching to make sure we got the job done." I release the man and get to my feet, looking around to see where he'd be most likely to have positioned himself. The tactical team had been in place prior to the meeting and they had the best line of sites covered.

"You guys didn't see anyone else pull in here or in the surrounding areas?" I ask one of them as I try to think frantically of what to do next. The phone in the dead man's pocket starts to ring and I lunge for it.

I connect the call but don't say a word. I don't need to because the man on the other end of the line is already talking. "Nice show you put on. I knew she tipped you off. Now you'll never get her back."

"She didn't tip us off. When the meeting site changed I knew something was up. Then she wasn't answering her phone." Jordan is at this man's mercy and I'll be damned if my actions will cause her to be punished. "Just tell me what you want."

"You're about to expose me as a corrupt federal official. The only thing I want now is to get the hell out of here, which I'm well on my way to doing."

"I can still bury this. Meet with me, let her go, and we can make sure this thing never sees the light of day."

"I believe you'd be willing to do that, but any agency you had with you there shooting my guys today won't be willing to trade her. To them she's not worth it."

"Then take me instead. Trade her for me."

"Yeah, I'm going to trade her for the guy who was taking out my men from underneath a car. No thanks. Plus, I can have fun with her; I'm not really interested in having fun with you."

A few things run quickly through my mind. He can't be far if he saw everything that went down just now. Two, Jordan is still alive. And three, if I catch this man it's going to take every ounce of my willpower not to kill him. I turn as Maggie pulls on my arm and mouths silently to me that they're tracing the call and I should stall.

"Is that the only way a guy like you ends up with a girl like Jordan? You have to kidnap her?" I don't have to work hard to let the seething anger I'm feeling come through in my voice.

"Oh please, she's not worth the trouble. Especially now that she's not so pretty anymore. I made sure of that. Her looks were all she had going for her."

"If you lay another finger on her I'll hurt you in ways you never knew existed. This is your last chance to change your mind. Otherwise this day will end with me staring you in the eye as I steal the last breath from your body. There'll be nowhere you can hide from me."

"Tough guy, huh? Good luck finding me. I've known for some time this thing could blow up. I'd be an idiot not to have an exit strategy. When I'm done with her I'll make sure to leave her body somewhere you can find it. That is, if anyone can recognize her."

I start cursing as my fist clamps down tight over the phone and I hear Wes disconnect the line.

"We got a hit," Maggie says, pulling up the GPS signal that's just been sent to her phone. "He's about four miles from here. He's heading north."

"Want to come for a ride?" I ask Maggie as I holster my weapon and pull the man on the ground to his feet. He's got a bullet wound in his knee and he cries out in pain as I lift him. "Shut up," I bark at him as I slam him against the SUV.

"Absolutely," she replies as she pulls the keys from her pocket. "Just let me update the Tac Ops team. I'll have my team keep tracking the cell phone and, as long as he doesn't ditch it, we should have a line on him."

"I'm sure he will ditch it. Get the car and I'll be there in a minute." I grab the wounded man by the throat and pull him forward toward the dumpsters in the corner of the parking lot.

"What's he doing?" one of the tactical guys asks Maggie, but she waves him off. "He's got this under control," she assures them as she jogs toward the car.

When the man starts to fight me, I spin his body so I have him in a headlock and I'm dragging him, his feet trying unsuccessfully to dig into the pavement.

When we're behind the dumpsters I slam his body to the ground and come down hard with my knee to his chest until I feel a hard puff of air forced out of him. "What's his plan?" I demand, and when the man doesn't answer I pull my weapon and dig the barrel into his temple. "I will kill you. You aren't worth anything to me unless you can help me find her. So you chose, live or die?"

"You're not going to kill me," he snipes back as he tries again to get out from under my grip.

"I have killed so many men before you. I have the stomach for it if that's what you're worried about. Out here, behind this dumpster, it's just you and me and I'll make sure I tell a damn good story of why I had to stick this gun in your mouth and blow your brains out of the back of your head. I doubt they'll question me at all. Not for a shithead like you."

When he doesn't answer again, I pry open his mouth and jam the gun inside, smashing it against his teeth. "Last chance."

"Okay," I hear him try to say from around the metal of the gun. When I pull it out he starts talking. "He's got an uncle with some property near the Canadian border. He knows a way to cross without having to hit any of the checkpoints. But he has to go in the morning. He's got it timed against different patrols. So if he's headed there now he'll have to stay in the cabin for the night. The town's called Bleacher or something."

I stand and kick my sneakered foot into the side of his ribs. I'm missing my combat boots. Maggie is over my shoulder a moment later.

"He ditched the phone. Did you get anything out of this guy?"

"Yes, I know where they're going but we need to hurry." I lean down again next to the man on the ground and whisper, "If she's dead, I will find you and I will kill you with my bare hands. No jail cell will keep you safe from me."

"He drives a black Mercedes that's not registered to him. I don't know the plate number but it's registered under a dummy company of his. Energist. There are only two vehicles. This SUV and his." Funny how the man can't seem to tell me enough now that he knows his life hangs in the balance.

"What do you want to do for backup?" Maggie asks as she grabs her radio and readies to ask for more men.

"He's heading toward Canada. Put a BOLO on his car. This asshole says the name of the town is Bleacher or something. His uncle owns property up there so see if your team can track the address down and get it to us."

"What about more men? This team will need to be debriefed but with Bill's approval there can be another team on the road within an hour."

"Have him do it, but we're not waiting for them."

Maggie and I run toward the car as she calls out orders for someone to restrain the man behind the dumpsters and bring him in. I hear someone calling my name but I don't want to slow down. It isn't until Jonah is right on my heels that I give in.

"What?" I ask breathlessly through gritted teeth. "Why are you here?"

"Let them handle this, Click. Look at them; they're prepared. You can't go after her like this. It's too personal and you've got too much on your mind. I can't let you go." He makes eyes at me as though he's speaking a code no one can decipher. I know he's talking about the PTSD, but I don't care.

"You're supposed to be under agent protection somewhere. Who brought you here?" I'm too pissed now to sort out who I'm angriest at, so I just direct it all toward Jonah.

"They told me what happened. That Jordan wasn't here and I told them I needed to talk to you. That it was important, so one of the agents brought me."

"Jonah, I will knock you out if I have to. Look me in the eye—you know I'm serious. Our family needs you right now, but Jordan needs me." With a laser beam stare I finally get Jonah to back up a couple steps while I hop in the driver's seat and Maggie rides shotgun. "You're my *just in case,* Jonah. You're the guy that makes it easy for me to leave because I know they'll be all right as long as you're around." I close the car door and speed off as I see Jonah drop his tired head in surrender. Whether he believes me or not, it really is, and always has been, easier leaving when I know he's there to take care of my family. I'll never be able to thank him enough for that.

"At least she's still alive," Maggie states as she pulls the high heel shoes from her feet. "Thanks for not killing that guy behind the dumpster. I was sticking my neck out for you when I told them to let you go."

"To be honest, the only thing that kept me from killing him was he told me what I needed to know.

Otherwise you'd be cursing and cuffing me rather than thanking me right now."

"I joined the force when I was nineteen because my boyfriend and I were robbed coming out of a movie and he was shot and killed." Maggie pulls her hair out of the tight bun and shimmies out of the suit jacket. "If you'd have killed him, I'd still have let you go try to find her."

Chapter Twenty-Six

<u>Jordan</u>

I know Wes was talking to Click on the phone, but I didn't make a sound. Wes had already told him I was alive and I don't know where we are going since I'm blindfolded, so nothing I could have said would have helped him find us. Plus, I don't want my screams for help to be the last words Click hears from me.

Maybe I'm defeated because I'm not even trying to think of a plan to get away at the moment. I'm in too much pain to even consider what it would take to be free of him. Not to mention I have no clue where we are. I shift uncomfortably in my seat as the ache in my side grows unbearable.

"You brought that on yourself. Your damn boyfriend shot every single one of my men dead. Now I'm stuck doing this by myself." He's grumbling, acting like he's talking to himself, but I know he's trying to get me to respond. My gut tells me to lash out at him verbally but I'm trying to think less like me and more like Click. What would he tell me to do in this moment? He'd want me to hear the clues. To try to understand Wes and what motivates him. I know how to do that. It was my job with clients for years. He's still talking about something when I realize what kind of guy dates a bunch of girls at once. What kind of guy surrounds himself with a bunch of men to help carry out his plans. He's complaining in a worrisome voice about having to do this alone. And with that I see my angle.

"Do you know why I never called you back when we were dating?" I ask, cutting into his words.

"You didn't think I was the right guy for you. I wasn't making enough money and didn't have enough power to get your attention."

"That's not it. I thought you were great at your job and very successful. It's because I found out you were seeing those other girls and it broke my heart. I thought we had something and it hurt that it meant less to you than it did to me." I'm making my voice small and more passive than usual which is intentional, but the way I jump when he yells back at me is completely genuine.

"Bullshit. I don't believe you."

"It doesn't really matter at this point if you believe me or not. It's not like there is a future for us or anything. This situation is too messed up for that. I just thought you should know the truth. You were the longest relationship I'd had up until then. You understood me."

"I did," he agrees then changes his tone to an angry one. "Your boyfriend wouldn't be too happy about this conversation."

"We're really different people, he and I. He doesn't know what it's like to stand in front of all your peers and find that one game-changer deal. He doesn't understand the adrenaline that comes from uncovering the one thing everyone else has overlooked. I miss it so much." I raise my taped hands and scratch at the blindfold as if it's extremely uncomfortable and Wes suddenly yanks it off my face.

"Then why are you with him?" Wes sounds incredibly guarded, but I can hear him begin to crack slightly.

"I was trying to convince myself I could be someone I'm not. At the end of the day, whether it was morally correct or not, I loved what I did for a living. I was damn good at it." I bring my taped hands to my face and try to move my hair aside but it's too soaked in drying blood to be tamed. "I just felt like you not only understood that but you actually liked that part of me."

"I'd never seen anyone work the way you did. I thought you were so far out of my league. Like you saw me as just a chump who was toeing the line and being a good guy. That's why I was dating those other girls. I knew you'd call it off, and I wanted to look like I didn't give a shit."

"But you did?" I ask, trying to look hopeful and sincere.

"It doesn't matter now. Like you said, there's no future for us." I can see him glancing over at me from the corner of his eye, waiting for my reaction to that leading statement.

"Ouch," I groan as I touch the open cut above my eye.

"I wish you hadn't tried to get away. It's not like I enjoyed doing that to you."

"I know that. You're not that kind of guy. I didn't give you much choice. I was just scared. But can I tell you something?" With every word I speak the tension is slowly releasing from his shoulders. His grip on the steering wheel is loosening, and I know I'm on to something. He shrugs as an answer to my question, so I continue. "As bad as all of this is right now, there's actually a part of me that's relieved to be in a car heading away from there. Away from him. I was feeling so trapped and suffocated and, even though these circumstances are all screwed up, I still feel like maybe I'm meant to be here."

"Really? You can't mean that."

"I shouldn't have said it. Maybe I'm not thinking straight. It's not like we could do this together or anything. I mean, you have your plan, and I'm certainly not in that equation. I'm just confused I guess." I let out a heavy sigh and sniffle a bit.

"You'd try to get away the first chance you got."

"You were just on the phone with my boyfriend, and I didn't say a word to let him know I was even here. I could have screamed or tried to tell him something, but I didn't."

"So what? You'd just come with me and then what?"

"Start over? I don't know."

"Prove it." He scrutinizes my battered face.

"I can help you. I know how they'll try to find you, and I can keep us from getting caught."

"I've got that under control."

"Just hear me out. Where are you going? What's your plan?"

He looks at me while a battle of conflict rages behind his eyes. "I'm headed to the border. Once I cross over into Canada I've got ways to disappear."

"At this rate you'll never make it to Canada. We need to switch cars. Every cop on the east coast will have your picture and this car up on their screens by now."

"This car isn't registered to me. I've got a dummy company for this stuff. They won't be able to track it."

"When you pulled me in the car and I was yelling, I'm sure someone grabbed the plate and eventually they'll make the connection. Plus, the SUV you had me in first, the one your guys took and left at that meeting, was it registered through the same dummy company?"

I see a flash of panic buzz across his face before he answers. "Yes."

"Then they already know about this car, and I'm telling you someone will spot it. We need to get off the main highway and switch vehicles." I'm not thinking this will be my chance to get away. I'm just considering how to stay alive long enough for Click to find me. That's my job.

"But . . . I . . ." Wes stutters nervously. "Where are we going to get another car?"

"Pull into a mall," I say, shifting again in my seat as I groan in pain. "I'll distract the person and you take the car. We need something that won't link right back to us."

"You'll just bolt. You're looking for a way to run. I'm not a fool." His voice is sharp as nails and I have to force myself to breathe so I can speak.

"You're not a fool," I assure him as I reach my hand over to his forearm and touch it gently. "I promise I won't run." Wes got involved with the bad guys because he was overlooked in life and in business. His bravado is a shield, masking an enormous amount of loneliness and insecurity. He began to think the only way he'd get ahead is if he crossed these lines.

"We don't have much choice, I guess. If they know about this car we're bound to get spotted before we get to Beecher Hills. There's a mall about twenty miles from here. It'll be closing soon. But I swear if you—"

I tighten my grip on his arm. "I won't. But I need to get cleaned up first. Just a little bit. Is there a bathroom we can stop at?"

I see him flip on his turn signal reluctantly as he heads toward a rest stop. I steady my breath and take my hand off his arm. I know Click will come for me. I just have to give him enough time.

Chapter Twenty-Seven

<u>Click</u>

"I just got an update from the director. He says there was a report of a car stolen from the Pearl Street Mall an hour ago. The woman who handed over her keys said a dark-haired woman approached her. She described her as having a lot of injuries, and she demanded her keys and said it was an emergency. As she did so, the woman matching Jordan's description said, 'Jordan Garcia, Beecher Hills.' We had the property address for Wes's uncle narrowed down to four possibilities, but only one is in Beecher Hills. We're heading in the right direction." Maggie drops her phone down into the cup holder and hits the accelerator a little harder. "She's still alive, Click; that's good news. And we know where they're headed. The director wants to call in the local police department to go to the house now and be waiting when they arrive."

"No way, don't you have a tactical team to handle this? A small town police department isn't trained for a hostage situation the same way you and I are. They could screw up and get her killed."

"I know, I was thinking the same thing. If they left the mall an hour ago it means they have a three-hour drive ahead of them. They won't likely be speeding for fear of getting pulled over. They might even be staying off the main highways, which would slow them down."

"So what are our options?"

"Know anyone with a plane? The boss says there's a landing strip about seven miles from the property. He's trying to get a team ready but can't find transport that gets them there in time."

191

"Hang on." I fish my phone out of my pocket and call the one person I think might be able to make this happen. After few rings I hear Devin pick up. "Click, what's up?" he asks, sounding concerned. Devin is a friend who gave me a chance when most people would have kicked me to the curb. The time I spent with him in Clover was the only thing that helped me survive transitioning back after so many deployments. I saved the lives of people he loves, and now I'm calling in that favor.

"Devin," I say with a rush of emotion I didn't expect to have. "It's Jordan. We were working something through together, a big deal, and it went bad. Some guy has her, and it doesn't look good. The only chance I have at getting her back is finding a small plane that is ready right now to fly me in. There's an airstrip seven miles from where we believe he's taking her."

"Where are you now?" he asks, sounding like he's already jumping into action.

"The closest airport is about ten miles, in East Hampshire. It looks like a decent size strip," Maggie says after I switch the phone to the speaker so she can hear too. I don't bother with introductions; neither Devin nor Maggie seems to need the formalities.

"Yeah, I know it," Devin says eagerly. "I flew in there a few times when I had business in Boston. I've got a guy I can call who owes me some favors. Stay on this line, okay, kid? I'll be right back."

"Just start heading in that direction," I tell Maggie, and though she looks at me skeptically, she does. I don't blame her for not wanting to lose time if this doesn't pan out, but she doesn't know Devin and what he can do.

"All set, Click," Devin assures me when he comes back on the line a few minutes later. "There's a plane fueled up and ready for you. Flying time is just over an hour. Will that get you what you need?"

"Yes. I'll be able to be there before they show up and we'll have the element of surprise."

"Do you know how she is? I mean are you sure she's still . . ."

"Last update I got she was alive but injured. These people are desperate."

"What else can I do? Do you want Luke and me up there? We can get on a plane within the hour." The anxiousness and conviction in his voice remind me how impactful our time in Clover was for all of us. We're all changed, and for the better. I just hope Jordan gets the chance to appreciate it.

"There is one more thing, but it's a lot to ask."

"Anything."

"My family. They're involved in this. My brother-in-law stumbled upon some incriminating evidence against his company and they're trying to keep it quiet. We came to New York City so Jordan could bring in some of her old contacts to help us expose the information all the while keeping everyone safe. My family went to Jordan's beach house in Florida. But that was back before this happened, before anyone knew she was involved. Now I'm not sure that property is safe for them because Jordan is a link."

"I can get them to Clover and keep them safe," he offers, and I feel guilty because he has no idea what he'll be dealing with.

"It's a lot to ask."

"It's not. I have my family today because you saved them. You took a bullet saving Adeline. I want to help."

"But it's my four sisters, three of their husbands and all of the kids. And that's nothing compared to having to deal with my mother. She's impossible. She'll drive you crazy. You don't have space for all of them."

"Adeline will love the playmates. We'll put everyone up in hotel rooms and make sure they have what they need. I promise you, Click, they'll be safe. It's not too much to ask. Let me do this for you, and you go get Jordan."

"Thank you, Devin." I choke out the words and clear my throat.

"Get on that plane and bring her back safely. You got this."

Chapter Twenty-Eight

<u>Click</u>

Lying in wait. It's been an enormous part of my life as a Marine. Most people think Special Forces spend all their time in constant combat, but really, what we do more than anything is wait and watch. Timing is everything. Maggie and I have cleared the house, the property, and the parameter of woods around it. There is no one up here but us. The local police have been put on notice and told not to stop the car on its way in. There is a tactical team in flight, but they're twenty minutes out. By my calculation, Wes and Jordan should be fewer than five minutes out. They were spotted three times along the route to this property though police all followed orders and let them pass, acting as though they were completely unaware of the situation.

Now, as I lay on my stomach in the tree line just to the left of where he will likely park the car, I try to steady my breath. These are the moments I struggle the most with. It feels the same as it did when I was deployed. The cool metal of the gun in my hand and my body's position blurs the past and the present. The pitch black of the night in the woods makes it impossible to fix my gaze on anything that will ground me in the here and now. I pound my fist against my head and will myself to focus. I will not allow my screwed-up brain to keep me from getting to Jordan.

Maggie and I have a plan and I feel confident we'll be able to get the upper hand. We don't have any radio communication and our cell phones have no service, but before it dropped off, the last update we heard was the local police department had fallen back, are out of sight, and will have plenty of people in the area once Jordan is secure. If they hear gunfire they'll come running, but otherwise they'll wait for us to notify them somehow. We've parked our car a mile and a half down a dirt road set far into the woods and walked the rest of the way in.

I see two headlights cutting their way through the thick tree-lined dirt driveway and I know the rest of my life depends on the next few minutes. If Jordan is alive I will get to her. I will save her. But if I'm too late there won't be a person in this world who can save me.

The car rolls slowly, gravel and rock popping and crumbling beneath the heavy tires. When it comes to a stop it's about twenty feet short of me and I need to change my position to secure Jordan as she comes out of the passenger seat. *If she comes out of the passenger seat.*

The driver's door opens but only a fraction of an inch, just enough to set off the overhead light in the car, and I see her. Jordan's face is swollen and bruised but she's alive. For a second my life makes sense again, and then just as quickly that feeling evaporates as she leans over the middle of the car, catching Wes's arm, and kisses him. Full on the mouth and with a heat and passion that cuts at me violently. His hand comes up to her cheek and, as she grimaces from the pain of her injuries, he pulls away. Sweeping back her hair, I can see him apologize and run a finger over her cheek.

My world spins and I loosen my grip on reality and my weapon all at once. Could this have been Jordan's plan all along? This is her ex-boyfriend; maybe somewhere along this messed-up trip she found herself having feelings for him again. The passenger door swings fully open, and I see Jordan's two bare feet hit the ground tentatively as she coddles her injured body. That snaps back to the real world. Jordan left me clues at every opportunity. She wanted me to find her. She loves me and is depending on me to be right where I am right now.

Moving stealthily across the tree line so I'm adjacent to her, I feel the urge to charge toward her and pull her into my arms. But I have to think of Maggie. She needs a clear path toward Wes, who must be far enough away from the car so he can't reach for a weapon or drive away. Jordan shuts the car door and the limp in her step breaks my heart. As she moves toward the house, Wes is still fiddling around with something in the car, and I pray she stays right where she is. But she begins to hobble away. "Stay," I whisper, knowing I might compromise myself, but Wes doesn't react. Luckily, Jordan does. I see a tremble in her shoulders, telling me her emotions have just broken free. She stops in her tracks but finds a way not to turn toward me.

"What's the matter?" Wes asks as he finally steps out of the car and shuts the door. In an instant I see Maggie charge up behind him yelling, "Freeze." That's my signal to secure Jordan. I lunge forward and she stumbles toward my arms, her body going limp against me.

"You came. I knew you'd come. I knew you'd find me." She's sobbing out endless words that all run together like a train. I scoop her up, my arm sweeping under her legs and pulling her close to me, and move toward the tree line.

I hear a pop of gunfire and then silence. "You good, Maggie?" I call over my shoulder and hear nothing in response. "Maggie?" I see cars and flashing lights charging up the driveway and know the local police are coming. Once I lay Jordan down on the ground I stand and peer over the car.

Wes is on his feet and bolting toward the woods, away from the approaching police. "Stay here. Let the police know where you are."

"Don't leave," Jordan begs and I nearly let the fear in her eyes make my decision. But I can't. If Wes disappears into the woods and is never captured we'll spend our lives wondering if he's around every corner. I have to end this.

Rounding the car, I see Maggie sprawled across the ground with the handle of a large knife plunged into her chest. Her eyes are wide and lifeless, her gun still clutched in her hand. "Officer down," I shout as I point frantically to her location, and then, with more resolve than ever, I charge after Wes.

The woods are dense and the spirally vines whip my face as I plow through. Wes's white shirt is like a lighthouse in these dark woods and I have no trouble keeping him in my line of sight. There is a bullet in my chamber with his name on it if he makes the slightest move to turn and confront me. He's done enough to warrant it, but being a cop killer makes him enemy number one.

I close the gap between us to under ten feet and shout for him to stop and turn himself in. He ignores me and increases his speed, breathing heavily and grunting fiercely as he runs toward freedom. Unfortunately for both of us, it's not freedom in his path. My brain registers the cliff at the same time Wes's body disappears in front of me. I hear his panicked scream and do everything in my power to slow myself. But I'm storming forward too quickly, my body carrying too much momentum to prevent me from following Wes over the edge. I blindly grab for anything to slow me down as I go over, loose twigs and leaves offering no help. Finally my hand slams against something more solid, a thin sapling, and I grasp it with all the strength I have. It's no match for my weight and quickly snaps, but rather than plummeting over the edge as Wes did, I'm sliding down the side, crashing against the dirt and rocks.

I feel my body breaking, seeming to come apart like a boat hitting a reef. The pain comes all at once and then stops, which is never a good sign. Feeling pain means you're alive, you're not in shock. Going numb is far more dangerous.

Before everything turns completely dark I'm blessed with one moment of clarity. Jordan is secure. She'll carry our love with her. Devin will keep my family safe. Jonah will keep my family together. And they will all keep my memory alive. If I have to die, if I have to leave them all behind, I'm glad I'm leaving them all with each other.

Chapter Twenty-Nine

Jordan

Click's arms around me were like falling from the sky and landing safely, when you'd been convinced you'd die against the hard ground. But the feeling was fleeting, as he quickly released me to take off into the woods after Wes. I crawl my way out of the woods, calling out for help to the flood of police swarming with flashlight beams darting everywhere.

The first kind-eyed officer to run to my side starts evaluating my injuries but I shove him off. "My boyfriend, my fiancé I mean, he went out into the woods chasing the guy you're looking for. You have to help him," I plead desperately.

"Officers are already out there. They'll back him up, don't worry." He turns from me and shouts over his shoulder, "We need an ambulance over here. She's hurt!"

"Let me see her," a tall man in an EMT uniform says as he pulls off one pair of rubber gloves and slips on another.

"What about the officer?" the cop at my side asks with a look of confusion on his face.

"She's dead. Nothing else I can do for her. Now move over and let me see what I can do here." The EMT starts running his hands over my body, asking me questions that I don't answer.

"Who's dead?" I beg him to answer me and when he ignores me I yank down on the collar of his coat and force him to look at me.

"I don't know her name. She's an ATF agent I believe. Fatal stab wound to the chest. It went straight through her heart. Now please, answer my questions. Are you having any trouble breathing?"

I've never met this woman. I don't know her story or how she got involved in this, but I know she's dead, no more than ten feet away from me. I know Wes stabbed her and I know it could easily have been me lying there dead right now. Leaning back, I comply and tell the man where most of the pain is, leaving out that the worst pain I feel is coming from my heart.

As they start to load me into the back of the waiting ambulance, I plead with anyone who will listen to update me on Click. They lift my stretcher up and I hear someone shouting to hold the ambulance.

"Is she critical? What's her status?" a woman in an EMT outfit asks in a winded voice.

"No, she's stable, just some broken ribs and lacerations."

"Don't load her up then," the woman says, waving them backward. "We've got a critical one coming out of the woods now. He and the assailant fell off a set of rocks. He needs priority here. She can wait for the next bus."

I fight to get myself into a sitting position as I see three men hustling toward us with a backboard in their arms. A lifeless body is strapped across it. "Click!" I scream as I watch his bloody face pass by me on the way to the ambulance. I try to get myself off the stretcher but can't get out from under the straps. I know I'm screaming because I can feel the straining of my vocal cords, but I can't hear the noise I'm making. Two EMTs lay their bodies over me and try to calm my flailing limbs, but I just keep thrashing. Finally I hear one of them say, "Sedate her, quick, or she's going to hurt herself."

After a sharp pinching pain in my arm I feel my eyes grow heavy before blackness overtakes me. One last sob escapes my mouth as my body betrays me and reality vanishes.

Chapter Thirty

<u>Jordan</u>

The heat of the sun on my face awakens me, but I refuse to open my eyes. My mind is hovering somewhere between dreams and reality and, selfishly, I don't want to face reality. But the intrusiveness of the real world starts to elbow its way in. There is the beeping of machines and, as I flutter my eyes open, I can tell I'm in the hospital. Though I don't remember every detail, the first flash of memory is the sight of Click's lifeless body being carried past me and loaded into an ambulance.

"Jordan," a familiar deep voice says, and I turn my head to get a look at who is sitting with me. I see Devin's face come into focus as the clouds move off my brain. He looks uneasy, his eyes shifting toward the door and back toward me before darting away again. I clear my throat and try to muster the words I'm terrified to say.

"Is he dead?" Devin's eyes come back to me and the look on his face makes me think the answer is yes.

"I should get Rebecca. I told her not to go. She knows I'm not good with this stuff and I knew you'd wake up the second she left." His hesitation does nothing to calm my fears and a wave of panic washes over me.

I start pulling at the tube pumping oxygen into my nose and yank the monitors off my finger and the cuff off my arm. The alarms on the machines are beeping wildly as I start to cry out.

"Stop," Devin pleads, but his face is full of fear. "He's not dead. He's alive." He tries to reassure me as he clamps his large hands down on my shoulders, but I buck and fight harder to get to my feet. His words finally start to make sense to me.

"He's alive?" I ask, settling my body just for a moment so he can answer. "Is he all right?"

"He's hurt really bad. He's in surgery now, but he's alive. The prognosis isn't great though. It could still go either way."

I cry out again as I realize how bad Click's injuries must be. I hear the door swing open and expect nurses to come in and sedate me again, but instead I see Rebecca—a friend whose gentle face gives me much needed comfort.

"What the hell did you say to her, Devin?" she asks, her lilting southern accent in deep contrast to her forceful actions as she shoves him aside and moves her face extremely close to mine.

"I just told her that he's alive but they aren't sure he'll make it," Devin says in a panicked voice, looking like he might jump out of his skin.

"Oh gosh, Devin, just sit down and be quiet. Jordan, look at me." She forces my chin to align with her face and bores holes through me with her eyes. "He's alive. That's all that matters right now. Click is one of the strongest people I have ever met and if anyone can get through this, it's him. You know that. Any second the nurses are going to come through that door and sedate you again unless you calm yourself down. You need to be awake and alert for Click. Look at me," she says, shaking me gently by the shoulders, and it's enough to make her words sink in.

I pull in a few deep breaths as I try to focus. "He's alive," I whisper more to myself than anyone else. Rebecca's hand sweeps across my forehead, maternally brushing my wild hair away from my eyes. "Does his family know?" I ask, trying to get words out of my dry mouth. Like a good mother would, Rebecca reads my face and brings me a glass of water. After a few sips, I look back and forth between her and a still-nervous Devin for an answer.

"Yes," Rebecca explains. "Devin was in the process of getting the whole family to Clover at Click's request until we were sure they'd be safe. We got the call about his accident just an hour after they'd arrived and his mom . . . well, insisted doesn't seem like a strong enough word. She *demanded* we get her up here immediately. His parents and his sister, Bianca, and her husband, Jonah are all with him."

"I'm sorry about what I said, Jordan. You caught me off guard and I'm not good in those moments," Devin apologizes as he stands again and walks toward my bed.

"I know you're not. I'm the same way. I understand." Devin and I butted heads the majority of our time together in Clover. If you had asked me then I would have told you it was because we were so different, but I realize it's because we are so much alike. I don't have a history of being comfortable with emotions. But now, as my world starts crumbling around me, I know there is nothing I can do to protect myself from these feelings. I can't shield my heart from breaking; it's smashing apart as we speak. All I can to do is take comfort from having the two of them here with me and hope Click finds a way to survive.

Chapter Thirty-One

<u>Jordan – Eighteen Months Later</u>

Everyone told me it would get better with time. They've given me their advice and comforting words. They said every day I'd feel more like myself, and before I knew it this new version of my life would make sense. Advice is always filled with clichés, but I know everyone's intention is to reassure me and make me feel better.

Most days I actually agree. This new life is starting to feel somewhat normal. But just as quickly as I think that, I have to duck my head and cover my growing belly with one hand to avoid the serving spoon that whizzes across the long table, and I question if joining this family was the right choice. The advice from everyone is still ringing in my ears. Perhaps one day I will feel like my old self even in the midst of this chaos, but right now I'm not so sure

"Ma," Click yells as he catches the spoon before it can hit Mick upside the head. His reflexes are almost back to normal as he nears the end of his physical therapy. "Can you not throw things in the vicinity of my wife and unborn child? I don't need my daughter knowing how crazy you are already. She might not come out."

I let out a little laugh as Click rubs my belly affectionately. "I'm not giving little Maggie a choice. She's coming out of here sooner or later because I can't take too many more kicks to my ribs."

"Well I've told the fool a hundred times if he puts ketchup on my meatloaf he can eat it somewhere else.

This isn't a high school cafeteria for goodness sake. It makes a mockery of my kitchen," Corinne huffs as she raises her chin defiantly and reaches for another spoon. Luckily her husband grabs it first.

The table we're all gathered around is custom made. It had to be in order to accommodate this many people. The same crew that built the ramps to make Click's access in his wheelchair easier had offered to design a table that could fit this whole crazy group, and then a smaller replica for all the children.

"Corinne, cut it out," Click's dad says softly as he rests his hand on his wife's arm. "Today is a day to celebrate." He stands and raises his glass of wine. Everyone falls silent and turns toward him. "We're so lucky to have family and new friends here today. This last year has been a whirlwind, and while some people might look at it as a year better forgotten, I'm actually grateful it happened. Sometimes you need challenges and tragedy to remind you to appreciate days like today. Devin," he says looking over at Devin, whose arm is wrapped around Rebecca's shoulder. "Thank you for making the trip out here to Tennessee to celebrate with us. You've given my son so much, but the greatest gift of all is your friendship. The same goes for you, Rebecca. Your kind spirit and warm heart makes it easier to watch Click move to Clover. Knowing you'll be there with him gives us great comfort." Rebecca wipes a quick tear from their eyes as he continues. "Girls," he turns his attention to his daughters, "you all worked so hard this year to help your brother. You sacrificed your time and energy to make sure he and Jordan had everything they needed. I'm so proud of you for that. And Click," he continues as he chokes up slightly, "it's funny how you tend to protect your heart by keeping your prayers reasonable. First I just asked for you to pull through and survive. Then I started praying that you'd have all your mental faculties once you'd recovered. Once we knew you would, I started to pray that your spine injury would heal and you'd be able to walk again. And today, through an extremely difficult year of physical therapy, here you are walking around as though you were never injured at all. I've always been proud of you for the choices and sacrifices you've made, but today I see the strides you've taken to recover and restart your life, and pride is overwhelming me." He wipes at the stray tears streaming down his face and a resounding "aw" breaks out.

The warmth of the moment evaporates like dew on a hot morning when the kids begin arguing over who should get the biggest piece of Nona's meatloaf. "Enough, all of you, I made three more meatloaves. There is plenty for everyone."

"Nona," Adeline asks, and I watch Rebecca's face light up at the affection between the two. "Do you think if I eat everything I can have dessert?"

"Of course, baby doll. I've got four big trays of tiramisu and you'll get a giant piece."

Adeline's face beams as she starts shoveling bites of meatloaf into her mouth frantically.

I take one last look around the obscenely large table and reconsider everyone's advice. Maybe they're right. Maybe this new version of my life does make sense. And as strange as this bunch is, as flawed and crazy as they act—I can't think of anywhere else I'd rather be.

Chapter Thirty-Two

<u>Click</u>

I take Jordan's hand in mine and grab my cane by the wall behind me. "Want to go for a walk?" I ask, and her face radiates joy.

"Of course."

"Come on, Hemi," I say, patting my leg and the dog jumps obediently to her feet. Hemi has been a loyal and comforting friend to me. I'm not sure how I'd have survived some of this without her unwavering cheerfulness and constant optimism.

When you're in a wheelchair for any amount of time it makes walking feel like a blessing, and it's something I'll never take for granted again. Although I have to work through the pain every day, the ability to get up on my own two feet and walk out in the pasture behind my parent's house with my wife is truly a gift.

I'll be honest, when I woke up from the first round of surgery the pain was so excruciating I prayed for death. But day by day and little by little, life became a better option. Saying this out loud hasn't felt like a good idea just yet, but part of me believes getting hurt that badly was a blessing. The question of whether or not to reenlist no longer rages inside me. I couldn't now even if I wanted to. Fate has made that decision for me. More than that, the time it took my body to heal opened the door, making time to heal my mind. When I had nothing to do but lie there and drown in my own thoughts, it became clear the journey I had ahead of me needed to consist of more than just surgeries and physical therapy. If I was going to be someone worthy of being Jordan's other half, then she deserved the best of me.

Much to my surprise, after I was released from the hospital and was ready to transition to a rehab facility, it was Devin who stepped in. He had a medically equipped jet fly me to Sturbridge so I could be close to my family. Even to this day he swears it was the fear of my mother that had him making that call. He hired a private staff of physical therapists to care for me at the local hospital. I think some of it was whispers in his ear from Rebecca, but at the end of the day it was Devin who made my quick recovery possible. The one-on-one attention I received sped up the process.

As we step out to the edge of the open field, waist-high wheat all around us, I place a hand on Jordan's belly just in time to feel my daughter roll her foot across it.

"She loves when you do that," Jordan whispers, placing her hand over mine and resting her head on my shoulder.

"I hope I'll be a good dad." I've been debating whether or not to mention this fear for a while. Therapy has me opening up a lot more, so I am trying to express myself.

"Do you know why I'm not worried about that?"

"Why?" I tilt my face down to see her huge brown eyes staring up at me. I need her answer because I haven't been able to come up with my own yet.

"All a child needs is a parent who comes when they call, who shows up when they don't realize they need help yet. You always show up. You always come through. You do it for all of us, and I know you'll do it for her. That's all she needs. The rest we'll figure out as we go."

"I never thought I'd have all this." I gesture down at Jordan's full belly.

"Me either," she admits as she spins into my arms and squeezes me tightly. "For two people who weren't sure how to find happiness we sure stumbled into a lot of it."

"And I would give my last breath, I would fight with everything I have to make sure we hold onto it for as long as life allows. I will always come for you, Jordan. I will always show up for both of you."

"I've never believed anything more than I believe those words. Thank you for loving us so much."

"You make it so easy."

"That's a lie, but it's one I'll let you tell."

I lean down and kiss her lips as fireflies come alive around us. "Maybe it's not always easy loving you, but it's impossible not to."

"Are you two ready?" Jonah yells as he comes down the path holding hands with Bianca. "Devin says the plane leaves in an hour. We're all packed up and ready to go."

"I can't believe we're really going to do this," Bianca says, looking out upon the setting sun and shaking her head in disbelief. "Someone needs to pinch me because I can't believe we're really all moving to Clover and opening a dance academy for physically challenged and injured children."

"I can't wait to bring my sister and my mother down to see it," Jordan says, squeezing my arm. "After my sister lost her leg she was so sad she couldn't join dance when I did. It broke her heart. I've never forgotten the look on her face at my first recital. Dance Dreams Studio is going to be the kind of place all kids can come and feel good about themselves. We'll include everyone."

"It's like a dream come true for me. Thank you so much for letting us be apart of this," Bianca says, and she and Jordan break into tears the same way they have every time they talk about it.

"With Jordan's business skills I bet you'll be opening them up all across the country before you know it." I beam proudly at my talented wife.

"And how about you?" Jonah asks eyeing me skeptically. "Are you ready for your new endeavor?"

"I'm looking forward to it. I'll be responsible for transitioning the sheriff's department back into control of the law enforcement in Clover. I'll help ensure corruption is no longer an issue and things run smoothly as the security team moves on. It's really one of the last pieces left to regaining normalcy there. The town is thriving now that the recycling facility is firing on all cylinders. The economy is booming again. It's given them the opportunity to prosper and everyone has taken full advantage of it. I can't wait to be a part of it again. Devin has put a lot of faith in me and I intend to make a difference there."

"Oh boy, here come the waterworks again," Jonah jokes as he nudges me with his shoulder and I cry out in pain, clutching my arm. "I'm sorry, man. Are you all right? I was just kidding around with you."

"So was I," I laugh as I drop my cane to the ground and shove him backward. "You want to see if I'm healed enough to kick your ass, old man?"

"Anytime, punk." Jonah raises his fists up and we start sparing with each other. Hemi starts barking and jumping around us playfully.

"Can we leave the two of them here?" Jordan asks Bianca as they head for the house.

"I guess, but then who's going to remodel the dance studio for us to make it handicap accessible?"

"I'm sure we can find a couple of hot construction guys who can do *everything* we need them to," Jordan teases as she looks back over her shoulder at us.

"Okay, we're coming," Jonah relents as he drops his fists and starts following our wives toward the house. I take one more look at the pasture and watch the sun fading behind the tree line. "You coming?" Jonah calls back to me, and I turn to hustle and catch up to them.

"What about your cane?" he asks, making a move to go back and get it for me.

"I don't need it anymore," I insist as I shove him one last time for good measure and start the closest thing I can do to a jog toward the house. I pass Jordan and Bianca and though my body feels different than it did before the accident, the fact that I can get even this much speed gives me hope for the future. "Come on, keep up, you slackers," I call arrogantly over my shoulder and then promptly trip and fall on my face. The three of them race over like I'm a tiny bird that's fallen out of a tree.

"Click, are you all right?" Jordan asks kneeling next to me, though her belly is making that difficult. Jonah and Bianca are by my side on their knees offering to help me up, but I'm laughing too hard to even move. Hemi comes by and licks my face the way she does when she thinks I'm struggling.

"What's so funny?" Jordan asks, looking slightly annoyed by my inability to catch my breath as my laughter grows.

"I slipped in dog shit, and now you're all kneeling in it." Jonah hops up, followed by Bianca who has to help Jordan back to her feet.

"Oh this is so gross," Bianca screams as she looks down at her khaki pants.

"I think it's good luck." Jonah tries to comfort her as he looks down at his knees and twists his face in disgust.

"It's bird shit that's supposed to be lucky," Jordan yells as she hurries toward the house, and Bianca follows quickly behind.

Though my mother's love seems fairly boundless, apparently she draws the line at allowing shit-covered people into her house. Instead she tosses out towels and has my dad, who can't stop laughing, hose us down in the yard. The only person she lets in is Jordan who plays the "*I'm carrying your grandchild*" card.

When we are finally all cleaned, we have to race out the door to catch the plane, though I'm positive Devin wouldn't leave without us. Bianca and the girls kiss my mother goodbye and my dad pulls Jordan in for a tight hug. As they all step out onto the porch I hang back for a second as my mother breaks down into dramatic tears. It's just the two of us in the entryway of the house I grew up in, and I've left here a dozen times so this should be old hat to us.

"I can't believe you're going again," my mom chokes out as she pulls me in for a hug.

"Thank you for everything you do, Ma. Even the stuff we don't want you to do. Because I know not so long from now it'll be me up all night watching my child sleep. I'll be driving behind the school bus to make sure the bullies stay in line. It'll be me embarrassing the hell out of her for her own damn good. One day she'll be old enough to go out on her own and I'm going to have to let her even though it breaks my heart. And the whole time I'll be thinking about you."

My mother steps back from me and nods her head as she wipes at her streaking mascara. I expect her to say something, to impart some wisdom I can take with me now that we've shared this moment. But instead she just waves her hand slightly and watches me walk out to meet Jordan.

"Are you all right?" Jordan asks as she waves to my mother and we head for the car.

"It's different this time. Leaving I mean."

"Why, what's different about it?"

"Because for the first time I can't wait to come back."

The End

Author Contact:

Website: AuthorDanielleStewart.com
Email: AuthorDanielleStewart@Gmail.com
Facebook: Author Danielle Stewart
Twitter: @DStewartAuthor

Visit www.authordaniellestewart.com

Sign up to be informed about the latest releases and get a free download of Midnight Magic – a novelette. Also, every month a newsletter subscriber will be randomly chosen to win a $25 egift card.

Other Books by Danielle Stewart

Piper Anderson Series
Book 1: Chasing Justice
Book 2: Cutting Ties
Book 3: Changing Fate
Book 4: Finding Freedom
Book 5: Settling Scores
Book 6: Battling Destiny
Book 7: Chris & Sydney Collection – Choosing
Christmas & Saving Love
Betty's Journal - Bonus Material (suggested to be read
after Book 4 to avoid spoilers)

Edenville Series – A Piper Anderson Spin Off
Book 1: Flowers in the Snow
Book 2: Kiss in the Wind
Book 3: Stars in a Bottle

The Clover Series
Hearts of Clover - Novella & Book 2: (Half My Heart &
Change My Heart)
Book 3: All My Heart
Book 4: Facing Home

Rough Waters Series
Book 1: The Goodbye Storm
Book 2: The Runaway Storm
Book 3: The Rising Storm

Midnight Magic Series
Amelia

The Barrington Billionaires Series
Book 1: Fierce Love
Book 2: Wild Eyes
Book 3: Crazy Nights